MY MOTHER CALLED ME BEAUTIFUL

A NOVEL

by
Andre McNeill

MY MOTHER CALLED ME BEAUTIFUL.

Published by WriteIt2LIFE Publishing
www.writeit2life.com

Cover design by @Vikncharlie
Printed in the United States of America 2023

Print ISBN: 9798378612475

First Edition
1 2 3 4 5 6 7 8 9 10

Fiction > African American > Urban

Dedication

To my beautiful wife Adriane, my son Malachi,
and my parents
Pastor James O. McNeill and Lady Earlene McNeill

Acknowledgments

I would like to thank my gorgeous wife and my two sons for being by my side during the creation of this story. They are truly my heartbeats.

I would also like to thank WriteIt2LIFE Publishing for guiding me through this process.

Contents

Chapter One

It was the first of May. I remember it like it was yesterday. The weather was gorgeous - 85 degrees and not a cloud in the sky. The leaves were rustling ever so slightly in the trees from the calm breeze. It was the perfect day for my sister Abby, my brother John, my husband Malcolm, and I to be gathered together at the Westminster Gardens cemetery to finally put a headstone on my mother's grave. Although everyone was in a somber but grateful mood I couldn't take my eyes off of the most beautiful bouquet of red roses I had ever seen. The soft velvety petals smelled like wine and berries.

Malcolm brought them to lay over my mother's grave. I gazed ever so lovingly at him and I thought the gesture was so sweet of him. He caught my eye and smiled. Malcolm was my rock. He grew up in the same apartment building with us. He knew our family's plight from the beginning, and he always treated my mother with respect. Malcolm was two years older than me, but we became best friends. He always used to tell me how pretty I was, and he always treated me special. When he left for North Carolina A&T State University on a football scholarship, I was utterly lost. So I buried myself in my school work and my results paid off. My grades were good enough for me to attend Duke University. At least that was my plan after graduation before my mother took ill. I was offered a full academic scholarship. My Mother was so proud of me but her illness made the thought of attending any school nearly impossible.

The truth is ever since we buried her, I felt it was my obligation to put a headstone over her grave. My siblings and I couldn't afford to put a headstone on my mother's grave at the time of her death. Money at that time as well as most of the time was always a problem in our household. But I literally felt that my mother was smiling down at us at this moment.

My mother loved this time of year as the winters were a bit too brutal for her liking. You see she grew up in Haiti where the average daily temperature was hot enough to scramble an egg on the asphalt. I guess the heat was just in her bones. Although the four seasons of our home in North Carolina were mild, they still weren't quite warm enough for her. I remember her telling me how her own father brought her to America when she was just nineteen years old and left her with a Haitian family. She said he promised to come back and get her, but he never returned. My mother stayed with this family for a year. She earned her room and board cleaning patient's rooms at Moses Cone Hospital. It was there she met the jerk who turned out to be my father.

My Mother told me that she had a sister three years younger than her. For some reason there was a serious revolt in Haiti and her mother and sister were murdered. She bragged about our grandfather who was a high-ranking officer in the Haitian army. Aristides was president of Haiti at the time of the revolt and my grandfather served under him. It seems my mother's life in Haiti was full of happiness and joy. She and her sister had everything they wanted until the revolt. After my grandmother and my aunt were murdered, my grandfather took my mother and fled first to the Dominican Republic and from there to Greensboro, North Carolina.

My Mother died on April 28, 2016, at 2:32 a.m. of complications from A.I.D.S. and pneumonia. It was the hardest day of my life. The most important person to me was gone and in that moment I felt like the whole world had become my enemy. I had just turned eighteen years old, my sister Abby was fifteen, and my brother John was thirteen. We were not babies but I don't know if there is such a thing as a good age to lose a parent. One thing was for sure, we all missed her. There was an ache in our hearts that wouldn't go away and the memories of her just seemed to make that weight heavier and heavier by the day.

About two years prior to her death, my Mother became extremely sick. She contracted HIV from a crack cocaine and heroin addiction and was constantly in and out of the hospital. My mother told me that it was my father who introduced her to the poison of drugs. The way she recalled the events that got to her to this point led me to believe that somehow she seemed to know she was dying. I felt like she was compelled to tell me the truth about her and my father's relationship, how she got hooked on drugs, and about the secret relationship she and my father had. I remember that day in her hospital room. I sat in the chair beside her bed looking intently into her eyes. I felt if I took my eyes off of her for even a second, I might miss something. My mother was expiring very rapidly as she struggled to tell me her story.

The nature of my parents' relationship was a lot to process but I had to admit, I was intrigued to hear anything she wanted to share.

"You know your father was a junior attending North Carolina Greensboro University when we started dating. He was only two years older than me and it didn't take long for us to fall head over

9

heels for each other. Not too long after we hooked up, we got a space together in a rooming house. It was in the perfect location between school for him and work for me."

My mother described their relationship as lots of laughing, working, and loving.

"Everything changed though after he graduated from college. He stopped coming home every night. Most times it was just two nights a week if we were lucky. I was too hurt to ask why."

While she was speaking, my mind went back to that time. I remembered after that we saw him less and less. What was even stranger is that my siblings and I were always told to call him Mr. Nathan and that is what we called him; not dad, pop, or papa -- names you would call the man you share chromosomes and DNA with -- just Mr. Nathan.

"Mr. Nathan... When you guys were born, I asked him what he wanted me to tell you to call him. He said he wanted to be known to you guys only as Mr. Nathan. I admit I didn't understand but I didn't want to make waves, so I didn't protest. I just did what he said. I thought you would think it was fun like a game."

She looked up into the ceiling and started blinking really fast. I could tell she was trying to keep the tears from falling down her face. Thinking back, even then it was painfully obvious to me that for whatever the reason he didn't want much to deal with us.

The years my mother and father dated were the years they ended up with the three of us. Even though my father was not an everyday fixture in my life, he was always around in some capacity helping my mother -- that is until she got sick. After that he seemed to just up and disappear. She shared with me that she never knew where he really lived. I doubt she ever asked him. I always had the feeling that she kind of feared him. I don't recall seeing her date anyone else until she became strung out on drugs. The hardest part of what my mother shared that day was the realization that it was my father who was responsible for my mother's addiction to drugs.

It seemed to be getting harder and harder for her to complete the story of their sordid past.

"The worst thing he ever did for me was give me my first taste of that smack. We shot up together."

She couldn't stop the tears from falling at this point. I reached over to give her some tissues. Just hearing the words made me cringe. Immediately my heart was crushed. Who wants to hear this about their parents? I sat there in that hard hospital chair barely taking my eyes off of my mother whose frail figure lay lifelessly in the white metal hospital bed. As I listened to the tale of this strange relationship, I was ashamed to admit there were so many times I wanted my father, whom I had to call Mr. Nathan, to stay with us and never leave. My mother managed to slowly regain her composure.

"...but your father was tall, dark, and handsome! He was six feet five inches tall with dark, wavy hair and light green eyes. Even while he was in college, he was a very sharp dressing man. He rocked it like he belonged in the GQ magazine. He was my eye candy and you and your brother and sister came out looking just like him."

I saw my mother's eyes light up when she talked about him. And I felt like at least this part of her story was the part that was bringing her some joy. I loved Mr. Nathan but I also hated him too. It was hard not to. When he came around, he always brought us nice gifts. He even took us to Disney World one year.

"After Nathan got me hooked on drugs we got high for years until he overdosed on speed balling on heroin and cocaine mixed."

I remember my mother taking us with her to see him in the hospital in the freezing snow and rain. The four of us would catch the bus, and we would usually all fall asleep because it seemed to always take forever to get there. Eventually my father got better, and we didn't have to take the bus to see him anymore.

"After his near death experience, he went into a 30-day drug rehab facility and never used drugs again. I never intended on using drugs and when Nathan kicked the habit, I wanted to kick it too. I needed a program just as much as he did..."

Her voice trailed off again, and she looked to be in complete agony trying to continue. The tears came back in longer streams down the side of her face. She shook her head.

"... but when I asked him if he would take care of you guys while I went away for treatment, he refused. After that he started acting shady and stopped coming around even more."

I guess he felt like he couldn't juggle us and the life he was so desperately trying to have without us. Whatever the case, my mother was heartbroken by my father's treatment of her. After all, he was the one who introduced her to drugs. He was the one who bought the drugs, yet once he got clean, he abandoned us and left my mother to deal with a horrible addiction alone!

After my father's departure, my mother's addiction progressed into a raging beast. No longer able to financially support her habit, she started prostituting herself. This was not just dangerous for her, it was dangerous for us as there began a parade of strange and crazy men who frequented our home. I remember wishing I had superpowers, so I could just blink those fools out of our lives forever. The effects of my mother's behavior followed us to school. My classmates began calling my mother a crackhead. It hurt me so much to hear my peers say such awful things about my mother, but they saw the pain of the existence we were living. Mother and her friends would get high all night and sleep all day. She wasn't working anymore. The hospital had to let her go because she called out sick too many times. She started selling our food stamps and renting out my brothers' bedroom to other crackheads. The police were constantly being called to our apartment and social services constantly threatening to take us from our mother. Even though it was rough, I'm thankful they never did. Looking back on things now, I realize that it might have been good if we had been taken away. I think if that had happened she would have gotten her life together sooner.

"Then when he found out how strung out I was and I had to turn tricks, he just stopped coming around, period." But after what could have been a tragedy within itself, my mother had a wake up call. I later learned this is equivalent to what an addict calls their bottom. It happened the day my mother caught my little brother John playing with her needle. It literally scared her so bad she never got high again. Talk about scared straight! My mother said she knew that day that my brother could have been exposed to her woeful sins by playing with that needle or God forbid something even worse! She knew the horrible life she had been living, and she desperately wanted to change. And change she did!

My mother joined an outpatient drug treatment program, and she faithfully went to the NA meetings the last four years of her life. It was during this time she found out she was HIV positive. Her disease had taken a toll on her.

After her diagnosis, my mother was in and out of the hospital. I used to cry myself to sleep wondering where Mr. Nathan was. He had to know what we were suffering through. How could he just neglect us? Didn't he know we needed help, and we couldn't manage on our own? Over and over again the questions plagued my mind.

"I'm sorry I didn't take your father to court or make him acknowledge us as his children and his responsibility."

"It's ok mama."

I wanted to be encouraging but I knew she practically worshiped the ground he walked on back then. She would never have done anything that would have made waves. She said my father taught her everything she knew about the United States, and he controlled her life for years before he abandoned us simply because she didn't know any better.

That day my mother told me everything about her relationship with my father, and then she begged me not to hate him. I couldn't believe it! My father, aka Mr. Nathan was a completely selfish jerk, and she wanted me not to hate him!

If that wasn't enough, my mother looked over at me and said, *"you forgive me right baby girl?"*

This time it was me who fought back the tears. I couldn't let her see me cry, though. I had to be strong for her. But I had already forgiven my mother when she had stopped getting high and all the addicts stopped coming over to our place.

That day when I was at the hospital to see her was the day she officially admitted Mr. Nathan was our father. It was amazing to me that she thought in all these years that I didn't already know. Maybe it was her memory or the drugs, I didn't know. I was just surprised she finally admitted the truth.

The last thing she said to me that day was,*"Irene you are so beautiful. I should have named you Beautiful! You look just like your grandmother. As a matter of fact, instead of calling you Irene, I'm going to call you Beautiful."* Even though with everything going on, the last thing I felt was beautiful, I couldn't stop the corners of my mouth from turning up into a huge smile and my smile made her smile. Two days later my mother passed away and life became a living hell!

Chapter Two

The homegoing service for my mother was very small. Only my sister Abby, my brother John, Malcolm, myself and Malcolm's sister Jada attended. There was also Mr. Thomas and Mrs. Yvette Yancey. They were a married couple who became friends with my mother during her recovery. My mother was doing volunteer work at the city's food pantry where Mrs. Yancey also volunteered. Mrs. Yancey and my mother became very close from the start. Mr. Yancey owned a construction company and was a prominent City Councilman in Greensboro. Mrs. Yancey was a very sweet lady. She always went out of her way to help my mother in any way that she could during the last years of her life. Because my mother had no money to leave us, the Yancey's paid the funeral expenses.

Mrs. Yancey never had children but no one knew why. She was certainly a giving person. She also was a terrible cook! I can't put it lightly; her food was disgusting! Her cakes and pies were the worst. I never saw anyone take a boxed cake mix and add just as much flour to it. The cakes she made were so stiff, they could have been used as anchors on a Navy warship. They gave me cottonmouth for real. And to think, she always watched the food network. Go figure!

Mrs. Yancey was a short, round woman. She had long hair that fell past her shoulders to the middle of her back. It was a little black but almost all gray. For some reason her hair always looked matted to her head. I often thought, "this woman needs a perm bad." I wanted to take her to the beauty supply store and introduce her to some creamy crack relaxer for real! But I was grateful for Mr. and Mrs. Yancey. With no other family to care for us, my mother left Abby, John, and I in the Yancey's custody upon her death. This was a load off of her as she didn't have to wonder what would happen to us.

Mr. Yancey was a horse of a different color and the biggest jerk I've ever met. He stood six feet four and weighed about 260 pounds. He was an ex-marine who had seen action in Vietnam. All he did when he was home around us was yell. He loved Mrs. Yancey though. He always gave her everything she wanted. Plus, she never worked. Mr. Yancey would come in from work everyday and Mrs. Yancey would run to him and give him a big nasty kiss. Mrs. Yancey would show her fat self off when Mr. Yancey came in. It totally grossed me out. I felt like they were too old to be carrying on like that! Mrs. Yancey waited on Mr. Yancey hand and foot for everything and there he was enjoying every minute of it with that proud smirk of a jerk look on his face! The environment was so different from the one I grew up in and I didn't understand it. I should have been grateful but I found myself hating Mr. Yancey after we moved in! I couldn't put my finger on why. I just had a bad feeling when I was around him. I thought he was creepy.

The Yancey's had a huge house with lots of rooms and bathrooms. Mrs. Yancey had all this old furniture throughout the whole house and it always smelled like mothballs! The living room furniture had see through plastic coverings on it. It looked like a museum in their home. They had a pool in the backyard that had never been used until we moved in. Speaking of that backyard, Mr. Yancey gave me the chore of cutting the huge lawn with his push mower when actually he had a riding lawn mower in the garage. Picture that! I didn't like that at all.

Those summer months went by quick though and I was able to attend Duke University that August. I was so excited. It had been four months since my mother passed. I had been in a fog during that time half hoping my mother would just come back to life to get Abby, John, and me. Being able to get away to school helped me cope with her loss a little.

The day before I was scheduled to leave for school, Mr. Yancey showed up to the house with a shiny 2008 Volkswagen Jetta. It was black with a gray leather interior. Boy was it pretty! Mr. Yancey told me the car was a gift from my mother so I would have transportation to get back and forth. Wow! I couldn't believe my mother actually saved up the money to buy my car. I was literally in tears. To know that my mother bought my car was really overwhelming. I didn't know how she even pulled that off. She was always complaining about how money was scarce. I was just glad I could come home to see my sister and brother anytime I wanted. The truth was all we really had was each other.

Mr. Yancey handed me the keys and gave me a hug. I promptly responded by pushing him off of me! He was hugging me too closely! It was weird! I had to tell him, *"I aint Mrs. Yancey!"* I thought he was trying to feel me up and down on the sly, but he wasn't slick. I turned around and walked away from him immediately! I could hear him laughing as I left.

"Old, nasty creep," I muttered as I ran off to call Malcolm and tell him the news. I wanted to tell Mrs. Yancey that her husband tried to feel me up but I was scared that would get us put out of

their home. I told myself Mr. Yancey better chill though before I tell Malcolm!

I had worked all summer at Wendy's so I could take driving lessons. I thought I was a great driver until I got on a road with seasoned drivers. I found out very quickly that beginners need lots of practice! I wasn't really into praying but I was learning fast how to pray to God while I was driving. Malcolm took me out driving a couple of times to help me but I scared him half to death and that was the end of my lessons with him. He came to the conclusion that I needed to get better on my own. Getting on Hwy 40 East to Durham was like a motor speedway to me. People would be driving so fast I'd be scared to death. Then I would pray to God for help and he would send a traffic jam! I would be so happy. Slow and steady was my preferred speed and I always left enough time to make sure I made it on time to wherever I was going. Freshmen couldn't have cars on campus so Malcolm got one of his friends from Durham to let me keep it at their house.

While I was making sure I was set for Duke, Mrs. Yancey was making sure Abby and John had transportation to their school. She didn't drive so she got her next door neighbor to drop them off and pick them up from school every day. I was happy that they didn't have to take the school bus. The kids were very mean on those school buses. I remember how I was treated.

Mrs. Yancey was God sent. She treated us like we were hers by birth. She took Abby and John shopping, to the park, and to different school events. She took the time to just sit and talk with them if they seemed to be having a moment. Keeping it real, I believed Mrs. Yancey wanted her own children. The way she handled us was nothing short of amazing. From my observations, I believe she would have been an awesome mother. It is still a mystery to me as to why she never had children. Trust me, I often wanted to ask.

The great thing about turning eighteen for me was that Malcolm and I became an official couple. Once he turned eighteen and I was still sixteen, he was concerned about people considering him an adult messing around with a minor so we did our best with the"best friends" front. I'm not sure if we fooled anybody. Those closest to us knew better. I really, really loved Malcolm and I believed he really loved me too.

Malcolm was going to school to become a pharmacist. I wanted to be a doctor. I knew it was not going to be easy for me though but I was smart and I knew how to hunker down and focus when concepts were challenging for me. But Malcom was also being told that he had a great chance to go pro for football. He always said that he wanted an everyday career in case making it in the Pros didn't work out. He always joked that we would have our own one stop shop; a physician's office for me with the pharmacy adjacent to the building for him. I don't know why he was joking. I could clearly see it all coming to pass.

Malcolm was a junior at that time and he played football for North Carolina A&T State University. He was a three-year starter, played the wide receiver position, and led his conference the last two years. Malcolm was what I considered eye candy. I learned that phrase from my mother. He stood six feet five inches tall and was 220 pounds of muscle. He stayed in the weight room.

I wasn't bad on the eyes either. When I got to Duke and saw all the black chicks wearing their natural hair, I let mine go natural as well. The guys were always hitting on me; Black, Caucasian, and Hispanic, but Malcolm had my entire heart.

Malcolm was really into God. His sister Jada, who was eight years older than Malcolm, talked him into going to church. Jada was saved to the bone. This chick loved the Lord! We would hear her speaking in tongues when she prayed at night. It sounded like she was calling out the names of cars in Japanese or Chinese. I laughed but not Malcolm. He would let me have it. *"You better be careful,"* he would say. He thought that "it" might fall on me if I didn't straighten up. I always teased him about it. It was all just fun and games though.

Jada didn't play either. She was very serious about her walk with God. Either Malcolm or I always received a sermon from her when we went to visit. And some of Jada rubbed off on her brother because Malcolm joined the college campus ministry at one of the local churches in Greensboro called the New Cathedral of Jerusalem. Having not been introduced to church, I must say that this church was always rocking! The beginning singing, which I was told was called praise and worship, was crazy good. Then the choir would get up and blow our minds. Malcolm said they were among the top five choirs in America. And the Pastor was phenomenal. The Pastor was really what Jada explained to me as being anointed!

Malcolm joined the church and he begged me to join as well. I had to ask him if he was really going to marry me because I wasn't trying to do all that unless he had plans to marry me one day. Malcolm said, *"Baby stop playing. You know I'm going to marry you girl!"* You see, I was still a virgin. My mother made me promise to wait until I got married to have sex. She felt that my husband would always love and respect me if I waited. I'm sure she was thinking that if she'd done the same with my father, things might have turned out a little differently. Malcolm and I came close more than once though. Well, ok more than twice. Alright, more than three times but who's counting. I knew Malcolm wasn't a virgin. He said he didn't understand that he was supposed to guard his body as his temple back then but he did now. He respected me though and I loved him for that.

Mrs. Yancey allowed Malcolm to come visit whenever I wanted. She really liked him. She said he was well mannered and she could tell he was raised right. On the other hand, I could tell Mr. Yancey didn't like Malcolm coming over. Malcolm would speak to Mr. Yancey and he would act like he didn't hear him. Mr. Yancey was a strange fruit. I really believed he was jealous of Malcolm.

Chapter Three

One Friday afternoon, Malcolm was at our house visiting. We had plans to go see a movie that evening. When Malcom arrived, he looked especially dapper and smelled some kind of good. Even Mrs. Yancey asked him what it was he was wearing.

"Oh, *just some Kush Oil,*" he told her very casually.

He was always very modest about himself and he was the perfect gentleman. Malcolm asked me how I felt about him getting a tattoo? Deep down I didn't want him to get one but I told him that it was his body. It seemed like everyone in our age group was all tatted up, especially a lot of the students at Duke. I was hoping that it was just a whim for Malcolm but I figured he was going to do it anyway! I certainly knew I wasn't getting one!

As Malcolm and I were headed out the door to the movies. I saw the young lady from next door coming up the walkway towards us. I'd seen her many times in passing but we never had a formal conversation. Well, there she was standing in front of me. She was dressed just like this 1970s black hippy chick. She had on a short blue velvet dress that fastened in a knot at the top of her chest. Her white boots ran all the way up to her thighs. She had on a big gold medallion around her neck and her afro was so large, it would have put Foxy Brown's to shame.

"Hello," I greeted her happily as my eyes found their way past her eyes and forehead to the enormous Foxy Brown size afro bouncing atop her head.

"Hello!" she responded back enthusiastically.

"I'm Irene."

Almost simultaneously she responded.

"I'm Grace."

We laughed together.

"This is my boyfriend Malcolm," I beamed.

Malcolm managed to get out a very dry, *"How you doing?"* and then he excused himself to the car.

Grace seemed not to notice Malcolm's diss and continued smiling.

"Mrs. Yancey told me all about you and your brother and sister coming to live with her."

"Ok....," I trailed off wondering why Mrs. Yancey hadn't mentioned Grace to us.

"I just came over to invite you and...," she turned towards the car.

"Malcolm," I sang.

"Yes - Malcolm - to my birthday party. I'm having it downtown on the North Carolina Greensboro campus that night."

"Wow, thank you. That is so thoughtful and kind of you. I would love to but Malcolm and I are headed to see a movie."

I thought to myself, "This chick seems very interesting."

"No problem, maybe we can get together sometime this weekend?"

She was starting to look a little anxious to get together with me.

"That sounds like a plan. Maybe Sunday?"

Grace gave the thumbs up.

"Sunday it is. Enjoy your movie."

"Thank you! Have fun at your party and Happy Birthday!"

I waved as she walked away and proceeded to Malcolm's car.

"Why did she have to say North Carolina Greensboro University?" I mumbled on my way down the sidewalk.

I was immediately reminded of my no-good father! He graduated from there. I quickly jumped in the car anxious to begin our date night. Honestly, I would have loved to have gone to that party. I had never been to one yet and especially on campus. My curfew at the Yancey's wouldn't permit it to happen anyway. I had to be in by midnight. I was told those parties were just getting started at midnight! Malcolm lived on campus and he concurred that there was a party on campus every weekend. I knew he went to some of them but he never talked about them. It was cool though. I really didn't want to hear about His partying in any way!

As Malcolm drove away, we saw Mr. Yancey pulling in the driveway. He had this real nice pearl white Mercedes SUV. He was always dressed in expensive suits. Being on the City Council Board and the owner of his own construction company made Mr. Yancey very prominent in the community. Malcolm and I waved as we passed by. It looked like he shook his head like he was disgusted with us for some reason. Who knows what he was thinking.

Before we were clear of the house, I happened to look up to the second floor window at the room Abby and I slept in. She was looking out of the window and I waved to her too. Abby waved back, hesitantly it seemed. I figured it was because she wanted to go with us or something.

Abby was a straight A student in school. She was also very quiet most of the time staying to herself to read. She had these big pretty green eyes like our father, Mr. Nathan. But there was a sadness in the way Abby looked out of the window that kind of bothered me all night. I even mentioned it to Malcolm. He said that I should talk to Abby when I got home. When Malcolm suggested that, I decided that I was going to buy Abby a cell phone. Then I could stay in touch with her and John all the time.

Given our circumstances, I tried to talk to Abby and John a lot. I shared with them some of the good things our mother instilled in me. Abby was becoming this beautiful young lady right before my eyes. I wasn't that developed when I was sixteen. I remember when Abby was much younger she would constantly rock herself as if she were sitting in a rocking chair. I believe that the rocking had something to do with my mother's addiction early on. Abby still rocks occasionally, but when she does, I tell her, *"Abby stop rocking."* I think she does it subconsciously because she always looks at me and smiles and then she stops.

Abby had her first menstrual cycle while I was away at school. It literally freaked her out! I was so upset with myself because I didn't prepare her or warn her about what to do when that day came. With everything going on, it totally slipped my mind to make a doctor's appointment for her. I was thinking that Abby's period came later than usual for a girl her age. I was fortunate. Our mother prepared me for my first one and it still was a little traumatic. Eventually I was able to calm her down. I explained to her that it was natural, that it would happen every month, and that she must do certain things to take care of her body. I told her that it was all a part of growing into womanhood. It was hard for me to tell her things about growing into a woman. It made me miss my mother even more. Even while my mother was terribly sick for the last four years of her life, she took the time to shower us with the love, care, and concern of a loving mother.

At fourteen, John was already tall for his age. I think the last time he was measured he was six feet two inches tall. Our father, Mr. Nathan was very tall as well. John loved sports and watching WWE wrestling on TV. It was a great fit because Mrs. Yancey loved to watch wrestling as well. Hearing her and John watching it on TV, you would think they were wrestling themselves! Mrs. Yancey even took John and Abby downtown to the Colosseum to see WWE live. John was so psyched but Abby could have cared less. Mrs. Yancey just liked looking at the wrestlers in their tights to hear Abby tell it. Mrs. Yancey bought John just about every wrestling action figure there was. He had about 40 of them at last count. John liked the wrestler *Roman Reigns* the best. That was his favorite. Mrs. Yancey even signed John up for the recreation basketball team. John loved to play basketball. When Malcolm had free time, he would take John to the basketball court around the corner and stay for hours. Sometimes I would go with them. I was so glad that Malcolm and John were fond of each other and that Malcolm was never too busy to spend time with John. That's when Malcolm explained to John about the importance of getting good grades, staying focused, and not getting caught up with drugs or gangs. He was like his big brother.

John loved going to Malcolm's football games and Abby was just as fond of Malcolm as John. Malcolm always knew I would be a package deal if he wanted to date me, especially when my mom passed. I did my best to keep my siblings out of the vicious world that awaited them full of drugs, crime, and other awful things. My mother warned me that addiction was always doing its pushups. So, I would always have to do mine in defense of it. I fully understood what she meant by that. I vowed that I nor my siblings would ever live in that crazy lifestyle again if I could help it! I knew they still remembered the shenanigans my mother caused.

I made sure John and Abby stayed focused on school like I had done. John said he wanted to design cars. He was always changing his mind though. I told them with great grades and hard work, they could be whatever they wanted to be. My mother used to tell me that all the time.

I think John had a little crush on a little girl in his class. He only talked about that with Malcolm but of course Malcolm tells me everything. I'm glad Malcolm could tell and show him how to respect little girls! After all, our no-good, absentee father, Mr. Nathan, was nowhere to be found. I figured Mr. Yancey would have spent a little time with John too but he was not making an effort to bond. He would come home in time for dinner and then go straight to his leather recliner in the living room and turn on the tv. Oh well! Thank God for my honey Malcolm!

Once we were clear of the house, Malcolm asked, *"So what did the weird looking chick from next door want?"*

"Oh, she is having a birthday party at the North Carolina Greensboro Campus and invited us to come. I told her we already had plans for the evening."

"She looks very different."

"How so?"

"She looks like she's a lesbian and you need to be careful if she starts coming around."

I tore into him immediately.

"So what if she is, I'm not!"

"I know what I see and I'm just telling you to be careful."

I didn't see that coming! I thought Malcolm read into the chick a little too deeply and I thought it was uncalled for. Plus, I felt I needed some friends other than him. I literally hadn't really had any friends my entire life. My mother always needed my help around the house and I had to take care of her the last few years of her life! I knew not to get close to anyone in school and I knew not to let anyone get close to me. The years she spent getting high I knew never to bring anyone home! A lot of the kids at school knew what was happening in our home anyway. They called my mother crackhead, cluck, white cloud chaser, crack whore, chicken-head, and trick. My mother would act like she didn't hear them. Trust me, Abby, John, and I heard them and that hurt me to the core. When Malcolm heard them, he would threaten to beat their tails! They would hush then. They were afraid of Malcolm. Even though Malcom knew of my mother's drug addiction and her terrible ways, he always respected her.

I just let Malcolm's suspicions about Grace go. The last thing I wanted was to get into an argument on our date night.

"If you say so!"

I tried to sound convincing. I don't think he bought it for one minute. He knew me all too well.

Chapter Four

My first semester flew by. I was a good student so I had no problems adjusting to college academics. I continued the study habits I developed while taking care of my mother and I excelled. Before I knew it, it was Thanksgiving, Christmas, and New Years. It was nice getting to spend the time with Abby, John, and Malcolm. I even pitched in to help Mrs. Yancey with the holiday meals. I figured some part of the food would at least be edible! Honestly though, I pitched in because I missed my mother. We all did. It was our first holiday season without her. I knew it would be hard but I didn't realize how hard. I was grateful that Mrs. Yancey always seemed to know when one of us was having a moment. She knew what to say or do to comfort us. I was glad she agreed to take us in. God only knows what would have happened had she not.

Finally it was Valentine's Day weekend. The weather was brick cold outside and Mother Nature didn't seem to be easing up anytime soon! I had just returned home from a Valentine's Day get together at the Cathedral of New Jerusalem. Malcolm had succeeded in getting me to join. We had a really good time.

It was 11:30 pm. I always made it my practice to be in before curfew. I wanted to respect Mr. and Mrs. Yancey's rule to not *"be coming in their house all times of the night"* as Mr. Yancey put it. I pulled my shoes off and walked up the stairs taking care to step over the ones that creaked. First I checked in on John. He was playing video games on the cell phone I bought for him and Abby to share. I winked and waved and slowly closed the door back. He gave me the head nod and just kept playing. Boys! When I walked in mine and Abby's bedroom I was shocked to see Abby on the floor beside the bed rocking and crying. Immediately I knew something was wrong!

"Abby, what's wrong shug?" I moaned as I dropped my shoes and my purse to the floor. I grabbed her and hugged her as tight as I could. She just held me as if she were holding on for dear life and wept! I started rocking her and singing a song my mother used to sing to us in her native haitian tongue. She passed it down to me before she died. My mother said my Grandmother used to sing it to her in Haiti. The song always calmed us down.

I finished the song, pulled Abby's chin up so her eyes could meet mine, and asked again. *"Abby, what's wrong?"*

She snatched her face from my chin and buried it in my chest. Then I slowly heard her mutter out the words, *"Mr. Yancey tried to have sex with me."*

"He what!" I tried to keep my composure but I could feel the blood beginning to boil through my veins.

"He started sneaking in the room at night shortly after you left to go to school. The first time I remembered waking up and he was feeling all over my body! I didn't know what to do so I just laid there and acted like I was still asleep. One time he even pulled out his penis and tried to put it in my mouth!"

"That no good, child molesting creep!" Lord, I believe I went blank for about a minute!

"Irene, I'm so sorry. What are we gonna do?"

"Abby! No, no, no, my sweet Abby. You have nothing to apologize for. You've done nothing wrong!"

I reached for my purse, grabbed my phone, and immediately called Malcolm!

"Hey baby, what's up? Is everything ok?"

"No Malcolm, everything is not ok!"

I could hear him rustling around in the background. It sounded like he was laying down but now he was sitting straight up.

"What's wrong?"

"Malcolm, Abby just told me Mr. Yancey tried to put his penis in her mouth!"

"What!"

He sounded just as in shock and disbelief as I felt.

"She said he's been sneaking in our room at night since I've been gone. She's been waking up to him with his filthy hands rubbing all over her body!"

I heard more rustling, now, like he was moving around the room.

"I'm on my way!"

And then I heard the annoying "blip" sound the phone makes when you either lose the signal or someone hangs up on you.

I cleared the line and then I dialed Grace's number. Grace and I had become real good friends in the short span of six months. I learned that she was bisexual and she was leaning on becoming a full out lesbian. Malcolm believed Grace was already a full out Lesbian. Grace did try to kiss me once and I shut her down immediately! I told her I didn't swing that way and that I was in love with Malcolm. I wasn't curious about that lifestyle in any way nor was I interested in trying to experiment! I never told Malcolm. He would have gone ballistic! He already had suspicions and warned me to be careful of Grace. Despite her shenanigans, Grace and I genuinely became fast friends and Malcolm seemed to be cool with it. He always asked me to invite Grace to our church to which she always refused. Grace didn't believe in anybody's God. She considered herself to be an Atheist and to hear her tell it, she was not stepping foot in nobody's church.

She picked up immediately.

"Girl, I thought you and Malcolm were still out. Oh, wait, it's almost your curfew time. Are you still out? You need me to cover for you?"

"Grace!"

I had to almost yell to interrupt her. She was talking a thousand miles a minute and I couldn't get a word in edgewise.

"Oh…" her voice trailed off.

"Something's happened."

"Oh no Irene, are you in trouble?"

"No, it's not me, it's Abby. Grace, Abby just told me that Mr. Yancey has been basically sexually assaulting her since I left for school!"

"Abby, no! How could he!"

"Malcolm is on his way over. Can you come over when he gets here… maybe you guys come in together?"

"You ain't said nothing Irene! I'll look out for Malcolm and we'll be right over!"

"Thank you Grace."

I hung up the phone and glanced over at Abby. I could see the worry on her face.

"Don't worry Abby," I tried to sound reassuring. *"We're going to get to the bottom of this and everything's going to be alright."*

I was telling her something I didn't know was all together true myself but I was the big sister. I was supposed to have all the answers. I had always taken care of her and John. The truth was at that moment, I felt like it was my fault. I was supposed to protect them and I felt like I let Abby down.

It wasn't too much longer before both Malcolm and Grace were at the door ringing the bell. I didn't know how we were going to handle Mr. Yancey when they got there but it was too late to think about that now. And based on Abby's pain, I really didn't care! Mr. Yancey was going to be addressed about this tonight!

I ran down the staircase to let Malcolm and Grace in. Mrs. Yancey came out of her room appearing particularly disheveled putting her arms in her robe.

"What is going on guys? It's late. Is everyone alright?"

"No ma'am." I knew I'd be the one to have to tell her the truth.

"Mrs. Yancey, your husband is a no good, child molesting creep!"

Mrs. Yancey's eyes became as big as quarters and she yelled back at me, *"You watch your mouth young lady! I will not allow you to speak about my husband in this way!"*

She grabbed her chest, spun around as if in disbelief, and then she ran to the edge of the staircase and screamed, *"Yancey!"*

Mrs. Yancey sat down on the bottom step, put her hands over her face, and began to sob profusely.

Moments later Mr. Yancey stepped out of his bedroom in his t-shirt and boxers. When he saw Mrs. Yancey crying at the bottom of the stairs, he bolted down the staircase.

"Yvette! What's happened? What's wrong?"

I looked at this big, tall child molesting predator and I began to feel enraged! Mrs. Yancey got herself together enough to say only a few words.

"Thomas, how could you hurt these babies knowing what they've already been through?"

He seemed completely unaware of what she was talking about and he said as much.

"What are you talking about?" He was getting angrier. He stood up, looked right at me, and started yelling and cussing.

"You spoiled, ungrateful, menace of a child!"

Then that fool stepped to me like he wanted to jump on me. At that point, Malcolm had enough. He pushed past me and before I knew it, his fist clenched, his arm raised, and his fist connected with Mr. Yancey's face. Malcolm knocked Mr. Yancey out cold!

John raised his arms like he was declaring Malcolm the winner of a boxing match and hollered, *"Oh snap!"*

Mrs. Yancey's sobs turned into shrill screams! *"Oh my God, what have you done?"*

I was watching all of this play out in real time right in front of me but it happened so fast, I almost couldn't keep up.

Grace walked over to Mrs. Yancey and yelled, *"Shut the hell up! Don't act like you are surprised. You know your husband has a problem and he's had one for years!"*

Then Grace turned to me and her voice almost seemed to speak in slow motion.

"Irene, Mr. Yancey raped and molested me from the age of eight until I was 18 and Mrs. Yancey knew! She just turned her head and looked the other way and acted like things never happened in this dysfunctional house! Tell her Yvette! Tell Irene how Mr. Yancey got me pregnant when I was 15 years old! Tell her how you all threatened to destroy my family if I didn't get an abortion!"

Now it was my turn to scream.

"Oh my God, Oh my God!" is all that would come out.

Malcolm stood over Mr. Yancey's body that was still lying lifeless on the hardwood floor!

"*Irene, John, Abby, grab your things, we're getting out of here,*" Malcolm barked while never taking his eyes off of Mr. Yancey.

We didn't waste a minute. We ran past Mrs. Yancey up the staircase with Grace trailing behind. Despite my annoyance at Grace for not telling me any of this, I was glad she was there. She helped us pack up quickly!

"*Irene...*" Grace started.

"*Not now Grace!*"

I could tell she wanted to explain but now was not the time. I didn't know how long Mr. Yancey was going to be out and I didn't want to find out what might happen if he woke up and we weren't gone.

Grace and I quickly threw all of John and Abby's clothes and shoes into the suitcases we all had and the rest we threw in trash bags. We packed up my car and Malcolm's car. By the time we were leaving, Mrs. Yancey had gotten up from the stairs and was trying to revive Mr. Yancey. I was actually hoping he was dead for real!

We got on the highway and drove up 85 North towards Durham. I followed closely behind Malcolm. I had Abby in the car with me and John was in the car with Malcolm. Abby was quiet. I kept trying to reassure her that everything was going to be alright. I told her that I loved her and that I was proud of her for being brave and telling me what was going on. We had been driving for about 20 minutes when Grace called.

"*Girl! Ya'll left before the good part. Old Yancey is just now getting up off of the floor!*" Grace was laughing hysterically. For some reason she thought this was funny.

I could hear him yelling for Mrs. Yancey in the background to bring him the phone so that he could call the police!

"*Grace, is he calling the police?*"

She didn't answer me.

Then I heard her yell, *"I dare you, you punk!"*

"Grace, what's going on?"

Just then I heard Mrs. Yancey yell, *"Thomas Yancey! Have you lost your mind?"*

I tried again to see if I could get Grace to respond.

"Grace!"

"Irene, can you believe this piece of trash acted like he wanted to jump on me!"

I was still stuck at Mr. Yancey calling the police.

Grace had stepped away from the Yancey's now.

"Grace, why didn't you warn me about Mr. Yancey? You know I've always felt there was something creepy about him, I just couldn't put my finger on it. And you've known why all this time and you didn't tell me that he is a monster."

"Irene, I'm so sorry. I wanted to tell you so many times but you have become like a sister to me and I didn't want anything to come between that. And I was so ashamed. Mrs. Yancey was my babysitter when I was a kid. Mr. Yancey started molesting me when I was about eight years old. I was so young, I couldn't put into words what he was doing to me. Mrs. Yancey walked in on us when I was about twelve. He told her I made him do it and she just pretended like everything was ok after that. She didn't ask me any questions or try to help me. That's when he told me if I told anyone, it would be bad for my family. I felt so lost and I didn't know what to do so I started drinking. I figured if I was half out of my mind when he did things to me, I wouldn't remember and it wouldn't be so bad. Then he started buying me anything I wanted. As soon as I got my learner's permit he bought me a car. I totaled it while drinking. As a matter of fact, I accumulated three DWI's before I was 17 and I totaled two of the three cars he bought me having blackouts while I was behind the wheel."

I couldn't believe what I was hearing. I knew she had low self-esteem but now it all made sense as to why. It made me more angry with Mr. Yancey but it also made me sad for Grace. DWI's, blackouts, totaled cars. It was a miracle she didn't kill anybody along with herself. This was all too much for one night! But Grace wasn't nearly done.

"Mrs. Yancey quit sleeping with Mr. Yancey altogether so he brought in *prostitutes and other women for us to have threesomes. Then he got me pregnant when I was 15. I was ashamed to admit that I actually wanted to keep the baby but Mr. Yancey had Mrs. Yancey take me to get an abortion. He didn't want my parents finding out later on that the baby was his. Irene, I was real bad off, after the abortion I tried to kill myself several times! I took a bunch of sleeping pills one night. When I passed out, I hit the floor and caused my mother to come see what happened. I was rushed to the hospital and they pumped my stomach. I was admitted for a week and kept on a psychiatric hold and evaluation. That's how they discovered I was an alcoholic. That was just two years ago. Mr. Yancey hasn't come near me since then."*

For a 21-year-old, Grace had been through a lot! Heck, at nineteen I felt like I had been through a lot as well but my life seemed to pale in comparison to what she had been through. I felt really bad for Grace.

Malcolm signaled ahead of me to take the next exit.

"Grace, I'm so sorry all this happened to you. We're pulling off the highway now. I'll let you know where we end up."

"Irene, thank you for not judging me."

"Hey, we're family right?"

The truth was I had heard all I wanted to hear. I was officially grossed out!

Malcolm drove through a few stop lights and then we pulled into the parking lot of the Motel Six. We were about 20 minutes away from Durham in a small town called Hillsborough. Malcolm got out of his car and walked over to mine.

"You guys ok?" He looked in at Abby and she nodded and gave him a half smile.

"I talked to Grace most of the way here and she said Mr. Yancey was calling the police."

"We'll stay here for the night; at least until I can get my sister on the phone and we figure out our next move."

Then he opened my car door and motioned for me to get out. I unfastened my seat belt and slid out of the driver's seat. Malcolm closed the door and pulled me around to the back of the car.

"All the way here I was thinking about the best way to take care of and protect you all. Irene, would you consider marrying me?"

I blinked about five times and gulped.

"Malcolm, are you kidding me?"

"No, I'm serious. I know this is not how you envisioned your proposal but I think the best way to protect you, John, and Abby is for us to get married immediately!"

"Yes! Yes! Yes! I'm ready! Let's do it!"

We were too overwhelmed with everything that had just transpired to do anything but continue with the plan at hand. I reached up and put my arms around Malcolm's neck and hugged him as hard as I could. The truth was Malcolm and I had been together since we were kids. It was inevitable that we would be together. Malcolm gave me $100 to get us a room. I got us a room with two queen beds. Abby and I took one bed and Malcolm and John took the other. There was no more talking at that point. We barely got shoes off and we were all asleep pretty fast. We were exhausted.

Chapter Five

What seemed like only five minutes of sleep was actually only three hours. I was awakened by the bright glare of the television and the moving shadow of Malcolm's head shaking back and forth. He was watching the local news on the television but the look on his face was one of complete fear. I sat up to see what had him so troubled and then I saw it. They showed Malcolm's picture on the screen. The news reporter said Malcolm was accused of a home invasion at the Yancey's. The reporter said that Mr. Yancey reported that Malcolm stole ten thousand dollars in cash and a cache of jewelry. I broke the awkward silence.

"What! Mr. Yancey is lying!"

I couldn't believe he would stoop that low. But then again. He knew good and well that Malcolm didn't take anything from that house and it certainly was not a home invasion.

I started again. *"I'm sure his ego was too blown to chalk this up to what it was; Malcolm knocked your butt out and proved that you're not the big bad man you want everybody to think you are!"*

The news reporter told everything about Malcolm; that he was a star football player at North Carolina A&T, that he came from the projects, and that he ran with the wrong crowd. The story had Malcom looking like a hardened criminal! It was so embarrassing!

In all the reporting, Malcolm hadn't said a word. But after the segment ended, he dropped down on his knees and began to pray! I knew what that meant so I dropped down on my knees too right beside him. I grabbed his hand and I started praying too. I don't know what was happening but while we were praying, I believe I felt the power of God for the first time in my life. I couldn't believe it. Even with all the chaos going on, I felt the power of God through Malcolm's prayer. We always talked about what it felt like but this was the first time I experienced it for myself. I didn't know my man could pray like that!

Malcolm helped me up off my knees and put his arms around me.

"God's got us now!"

I looked at him and nodded my head up and down in agreement. I was still too full to speak.

"I'm going to step out and call Jada."

He grabbed his coat and stepped just outside the door. Jada was living in Massachusetts at the time. She had one of those jobs that often relocated her from state to state. I could hear Malcolm explaining to Jada what had happened. They talked for what seemed like about an hour. When he came back inside, I could see tears rolling down his face. I felt so responsible for everything that had happened. I thought to myself, "if I had just put John and Abby in the car and left, none of this would have happened." I couldn't cry because I was just numb and I was afraid. My heart was pounding rapidly. By now Abby and John were awake and they knew what was going on. They both kept quiet but they had looks of terror on their faces as well.

Malcolm wiped his face and cleared his throat.

"Jada is on her way to North Carolina. She is catching the next flight she can."

Before I could respond my phone began to ring.-

"It's Grace." I answered. *"Hey Grace, what's up?"*

I put her on speaker so we all could hear.

"I was calling to tell you two detectives just left my house wanting to know where you guys were. Of course, I didn't tell them or my parents where you guys are. They tried to threaten me saying I would get charged with being an accomplice to the crime. Girl, I cussed them out and told them there was no crime and that they are getting played! Mr. Yancey has my parents pissed! I told them he was lying to save face. They had the nerve to ask me for my cell phone! I told them to get a warrant!"

Grace was so comical, we couldn't help but laugh. With everything going on, we needed a little laughter.

"I'm so glad you held it down for us Grace. We owe you big time."

Malcolm chimed in.

"Yeah, thanks Grace."

Malcolm mouthed to me that he wanted to talk so I cut Grace off.

"Grace, we've got some things to hash out. Let me call back."

"Ok chicka! Bye bye."

Malcolm and I stepped outside to talk. He grabbed my hands and I was immediately scared.

"I talked to Jada and she isn't happy about how this whole thing has played out. Jada thinks under the circumstances it would be best if I turned myself in to the police."

I was too numb to respond with words but the tears that started to fall from my eyes spoke for me.

"No, no. Don't do that."

He wiped the tears from my face.

"We've got a plan that should keep us all safe, baby. Remember we're getting married right?"

I managed to get out a small, *"yes."*

That wasn't good enough for Malcolm.

"You haven't changed your mind on me have you?" We're getting married right?"

He put both hands on my shoulders by this time as he looked intently into my eyes. I didn't want him to split his wig so I belted out, *"Yes Malcolm, we're getting married!"*

"Ok. Just making sure you're not backing out on me."

"Not a chance," I responded, sure of that and only that.

"Jada said Mr. Yancey is taking advantage of the fact that he is a very powerful man in Greensboro so we have to get reinforcements that will be on our side. She is calling Pastor Murphy for us to explain what really happened and to see if he can marry us as soon as possible. And then we'll get my coach and an attorney to go with me to the jail."

Just hearing the word *jail* made me more afraid than I already was. I needed to do something so I wouldn't continue to feel helpless.

"Food!"

Malcolm looked confused.

"I'm hungry. Aren't you hungry? I know John is probably starving by now..." I trailed off. Malcolm was accustomed to these rantings in previous situations when I felt like this and he read my cues perfectly. He pulled out his debit card and handed it to me.

"I'm not hungry but make sure you get enough for you guys."

Then he gave me what looked like the last cash he had.

"You'll need to stop by the office and pay for us to stay another night too. I need to stay out of sight. I can't risk someone seeing me

and calling the cops, messing up our plan before we get a chance to get everything together."

I could tell that Malcolm was very nervous. I'd never seen him like this before. Even though I was excited about the thought of getting married only a couple of days after Valentine's Day, there were so many unanswered questions in my mind. I was overwhelmed by Malcolm's care of us. My mother always used to tell me love has no boundaries. But I was starting to feel jittery. There was no question of how much I loved Malcolm, I was ashamed that we were having to get married under these circumstances.

I grabbed my purse and headed out to grab us something to eat. As soon as I closed the car door, my phone rang again. This time the number that popped up was Mrs. Yancey. I stared at the phone but I didn't pick up. She left a message wanting to know if we were alright. I listened to the message a couple of times and I could hear it in her voice that she was genuinely concerned. I couldn't imagine being trapped in her world. I wondered if she was happy portraying Mr. Yancey as this wonderful man and upstanding citizen? They did a great acting job for sure. As far as I was concerned Thomas Yancey was a monster and a liar and he needs to be locked up!

As I was leaving the Hardee's with our breakfast, I saw three different police cars and I got paranoid. Even though we weren't in Greensboro, Malcolm's face was probably plastered all over the three major news networks in our area by now. I knew I had to get myself together and be strong for my man before I got back to the room. As I was turning into the motel parking lot, Malcolm was standing outside the room on the phone.

I tipped past him into the room. He reached out and rubbed my arm. I could tell he was trying to look reassuring. I smiled back so he wouldn't worry but I felt everything but reassured. Besides, I had to be strong for John and Abby. I took the breakfast in and fed Abby and John. John almost tackled me before I could even put the bag down. I knew his greedy butt was hungry because he stayed hungry. He eats like a horse.

I looked over at Abby, her eyes were swollen from a night filled with crying.

"You ok, babygirl?" I sounded like my mother.

She nodded her head up and down.

"I'm ok but sis, if it's alright with you, I never want to go to the Yancey's house ever again!"

Before I could respond, Malcolm opened the door and came back into the room.

"That was Pastor Murphy," he said. He looked better than he did when I left to get breakfast. Pastor Murphy was 50 years old. In addition to always giving us a powerful word from God, he was a very smart, wise, and intelligent businessman as well. I was enjoying going to church and had just started anticipating hearing his sermons every Sunday. Coming through the door, Malcolm overheard Abby's comment.

"Abby, if God be my helper, you will never have to worry about Mr. Yancey again."

He sat on the side of the bed and looked at all of us. He looked worn out from not nearly enough sleep.

Before I could speak Malcolm started, *"John and Abby, Irene and I have something to tell you."*

Abby looked concerned and John just stared straight at Malcolm and kept chewing.

"Remember I promised you guys when your mother died that I'd always be there for you?"

John and Abby nodded again.

"Well I intend to honor that promise in an official capacity. Tomorrow afternoon your sister and I are getting married."

John jumped up, pumping his fist and yelled, *"Yes!"*

Malcolm looked over at Abby and although she was still a little shaken from the night's events, she had a huge smile on her face as wide as a Cheshire cat.

"Jada's flight arrives at two o'clock tomorrow which gives us plenty of time to pick her up and get to the church on time."

Before he could continue his phone rang. It was Jada. I had to admit even though I was still a little nervous about getting married like this, watching Malcolm talk to her and put plans together for our future made him look even better to me at that moment.

The phone call with Jada was quick and Malcolm was able to continue.

"Jada is going to get another room here tomorrow so Irene and I can celebrate our wedding night. Under the circumstances, Jada, Pastor Murphy, and I think it will be best if you all go back to Massachusetts with Jada immediately to live for a while. Jada feels it will be better for us."

I must say, I was in complete shock. I mean I'd agreed to the wedding but leaving North Carolina.

"Wow, I will have to leave Duke!" I didn't want to sound selfish but I had worked hard to secure the full scholarship I'd received to get to go to Duke. More questions swirled around in my mind. Would I lose my scholarship? Could it be transferred to Massachusetts? Jada was in Massachusetts for her job, what happens if they move her somewhere else? Will we go with her? Oh, I was getting a headache.

"Yes, for the time being. Jada is going to help you get custody of John and Abby. We will all be staying with Jada until I get us our

own place. Jada knows a lot of people in Massachusetts and she will help us to get everything we need."

"Good gracious, we are moving fast!" I hoped I didn't sound ungrateful but I was truly in my feelings at this moment.

"I know, I know. It's just that when I turn myself in, I don't know how long I'm going to be detained. And Jada and I agree that you shouldn't visit until you officially get custody of John and Abby. Social Services will be looking for you all because you are considered foster children awarded to the Yancey's!"

"Wow, Massachusetts!" was all I could muster out.

I smiled and tried to look excited but I was immediately worried how we would all adjust to living in a new state we've never been to before. I'd only been out of North Carolina once and that was when Mr. Nathan took my mother, Abby, John, and I to Orlando, Florida to Disneyland. I remember the ride to Orlando felt like forever. But once we arrived I didn't want to come back to North Carolina. For those three days, I felt like I was in heaven. I fooled myself into thinking we were a family now with Mr. Nathan in Florida! Of course once we arrived back in North Carolina that great family feeling quickly dissipated and it was back to our grim reality. Mr. Nathan promptly dropped us off at our apartment and left.

Malcolm's cell started ringing again. His coach and friends were calling to see if he was all right. Malcolm's friends wanted to go beat Mr. Yancey themselves but Malcolm told them not to do that! It would only make matters worse. Malcolm said he felt like this was a God-case and he wanted God to handle this! Even though I was new to the church scene, I figured in order for it to work, I had to believe in God even more too!

Chapter Six

We managed to get better sleep that night. Right before I drifted off, Abby asked me if I was excited to be getting married. She was so cute. She pulled the cover over our heads and we talked and giggled like we did when my mother was alive. I held back the tears when I thought of my mother. I was getting married without her. Then I thought would she be happy this was all happening right now? She wanted so much for me to finish college. I would be the first one in our family. But she would be proud that Malcolm and I were doing what we thought was best to keep our family together.

When I opened my eyes, I realized that I was the last one awake. John and Abby were watching tv and Malcolm looked like he had been watching me sleep.

"*Malcolm!*"

"*What?*" He was so mischievous.

"*Were you watching me sleep?*"

"*Why? Can't a man watch the woman who is about to be his wife sleep?*"

John and Abby laughed. Wife. I was still nervous about that word. Although Malcolm and I had been together forever, in just a few hours I would officially be his wife. I was scared about what that looked like. So far I had not had a good example. My mother and Mr. Nathan never married but they had three children. Mrs. Yancey was my only other example but she covered Mr. Yancey's sins and that wasn't right so she didn't qualify for a good example of a wife either. I didn't want Malcolm to suspect my apprehension so I gave him a love pat on my way to the bathroom.

"Yes, that would be Mrs. Irene Austin to you sir!" as I skipped past trying to out run his reach.

Jada's flight landed at 2 p.m. in Raleigh and Malcolm and I were there to pick her up. She looked concerned but definitely happy to see us.

"What am I going to do with the two of you?" she asked lovingly as she slid into the backseat of the car.

As we drove back to the hotel we all discussed the game plan in detail so we would all be on the same page. Malcolm had spoken to Jada about everything but because we hadn't been able to be alone, we waited until we were somewhere John and Abby couldn't hear us. We didn't want them to worry and I knew from taking care of my mother that questions that are unable to be answered create more problems than it's worth.

When we arrived back at the hotel and Jada was checked in and settled, she called me to her room.

"We haven't had any time to talk with everything going on. I know this is tough for you with everything that's happened. You don't have Mrs. Yancey and your mother is not around. How are you holding up?"

I was finally glad to be able to talk out some of my fears and insecurities with someone I could trust.

"To be honest, I'm terrified! I know I love Malcolm and he loves me but I want to be a good wife and I'm scared I haven't had the

best example of one. I was hoping to learn from Mrs. Yancey... some example she turned out to be. I just don't want to let Malcolm down."

Jada put her hand over mine and tried to reassure me.

"Irene, you're putting way too much pressure on yourself. If there's one thing I know about you, it's that you're resilient. You've been able to bounce back from challenges most of your life. You have a very strong sense of yourself. Don't discount that. You made the most important decision of your life when you gave your life to Christ. I know you're still a new convert but you can trust God to bring you out of this too. You're not alone. Yes we're with you but most importantly God is with you and when He's with us, we cannot fail. Because God is the greatest power, we cannot be defeated. Do you believe that?"

The tears had begun to spill down my face. I really needed to hear what Jada was saying to me. I'd had no encouragement from anyone and the weight of our situation has already become cumbersome to bear.

I nodded my head, "yes I believe that."

Jada reached out and hugged me and I felt like a weight had been lifted. I still had some uncertainties but I was more encouraged to trust in Jesus.

As she handed me some tissues, I managed to squeak out, "Thank you Jada," I wanted her to know how much I appreciated her.

"No worries. That's what sisters are for!" Jada appeared to be extremely happy.

I thought we had concluded our conversation but Jada said one more thing. She walked to the closet and unzipped a garment bag and pulled out the prettiest white dress I'd ever seen! It had lace that folded into the dress in a classic design!

"Jada!" I screamed now with my own excitement.

"You didn't!"

She replied, *"I knew you've been holed up in this hotel and you didn't have time to do anything for today, much less get a dress."*

"You shouldn't have! But I'm sure glad you did. I'm not even going to lie. I love it!"

"It was nothing. I grabbed it on the way to the airport."

I was more happy about getting married now. I had a beautiful white dress! That's more than I'd imagined I would have.

I got dressed in Jada's room. I didn't stress about something borrowed or something blue. I had a beautiful new dress and my mother's pearl earring and necklace set.

Malcolm was waiting for me when I walked out Jada's room to the car. He had the biggest smile I'd ever seen.

"You are beautiful!" he said as he opened the door for me to get in.

"You look very handsome yourself Mr. Austin."

He escorted me to the driver's seat. We didn't want to risk Malcolm being seen so we put him in the backseat between John and Abby. Of course, they thought it was hilarious.

We drove back to Greensboro and at 6 p.m., we were all standing at the altar of our church; there was our Pastor, Jada, two of Malcolm's best friends, Malcolm's coach, Grace, Abby, John and me. Pastor didn't take long either. The ceremony was quick and just like that we were married for real! Even in the midst of everything going on I felt like a queen for a day. Truth be told, with everything going on I really needed to feel like this at this point. I felt my mother up in heaven smiling, calling me by her nickname for me, "Beautiful." This was an awesome feeling and I didn't want it to end. Strangely though, I secretly wished Mr. Nathan could have been here to give me away! It was a fleeting thought, though. I figured I should stop bugging on him and enjoy my moment! Afterall, I didn't know how long Malcolm and I would be separated from each other after today. I actually dreaded thinking about it.

Once the ceremony was over, we were given meals to take with us that were prepared by the church culinary ministry. I couldn't wait to get into it. It smelled so good. Those seasoned women could cook! If anyone was happy about the food, I knew it would be John. All I could think was that this was so nice of our Pastor to pull all of this together and at a real short notice! It just made the day feel even more special. Malcolm always said that our Pastor was a full five-fold Pastor always making sure the needs of his people were met in every capacity. I was glad I joined.

We said our goodbyes and headed back to the motel. John and Abby headed off to Jada's room leaving Malcolm and I alone. All I could think about was wow, I am married now and I was so scared! I was still a virgin and Grace had already been teasing me about my wifely duties on my first night as Malcolm's wife. I needed my momma for real now! My emotions were all over the place. I had to laugh at myself.

Malcolm wanted to get right down to business but I still had so many questions running through my mind. Malcolm had only one.

"Are you going to be loyal and wait for me Irene?

"Malcolm, of course I am! You're my husband now. Wasn't that what we said in our vows?" I wanted to sound reassuring for him.

He grabbed me and kissed me like he had never kissed me before and the rest was the sum total of an amazing night with my husband. All I can say is once we got going, it was ahh sooky sooky from there! I was already prepared to yell, "hush Grace!" in my head and I hadn't even talked to her yet.

We slept peacefully through the night. I kept waking up wishing that the night would never end. I knew what lay ahead in the morning. Malcolm was turning himself in to the police and John, Abby, and I were about to embark on a whole new life in Massachusetts. It felt like life was traveling at warp speed and I was powerless to slow it down.

The morning came too quickly. We woke up and greeted each other.

"Good morning Mrs. Austin," Malcolm almost sang.

"Good morning Mr. Austin!"

I couldn't help but smile. It felt wonderful and surreal at the same time.

"We better get packing. Everyone will be here soon. " Malcolm jumped out of the bed and sauntered to the shower.

I pulled out all of the clothes we'd worn and packed them up in the suitcases. Many of the clothes we had were brand new. Mrs. Yancey had taken us shopping early on and basically replaced our whole wardrobes. Looking at the clothes now, I felt sad. Everything was going so well. Why did Mr. Yancey have to mess it up!

No sooner than we were dressed and packed up, our Pastor and Malcolm's coach were there to pick him up. We were all gathered together in the room.

Pastor Murphy said, *"Let's grab hands and pray."*

Pastor Murphy, Jada, Coach Richards, Abby, John, Malcolm, and I formed a circle and joined hands. Pastor Murphy began to pray. When he finished we were all in tears! There wasn't a dry eye in the room. Even Coach Richards teared up! Pastor Murphy and Coach Richards went to wait in the car while we all said our goodbyes to Malcolm. Abby, Jada, and I couldn't stop crying. We were a mess!

Once we got outside together we started taking pictures with our cells together for a good ten minutes! Jada, John, and Abby stepped away and Malcolm and I just hugged for a few minutes. We held onto each other for dear life.

Malcolm whispered in my ear, *"God is going to bring us out of this crazy mess. I promise!"*

I had to admit, I wasn't feeling that at all! But I was just learning to trust God and stand on His Word. Jada came over and hurried us along.

"Come on you two. It's time to go."

Malcolm held on for one more minute and said, *"I love you Irene."*

With the tears still running down my face, I managed to squeak out, *"I love you too Malcolm."*

He walked me over to the car and shut my door. He waved goodbye to us and ran over to get in the car with Pastor Murphy and Coach Richards. They drove off and the realization that Malcolm was gone coupled with the fact that Abby, John, and I were leaving our life in Greensboro behind, the place that we were born and reared became almost too much to bear. I tried not to sob but I couldn't stop. John and Abby told me that I'd have to stop crying so I could see to drive but I think I cried the whole day!

Before we hit the highway, Jada took me to get a quick oil change! She got the oil changed on Malcolm's car as well as we were taking it to Massachusetts with us. From there we went to the gas station, filled up, and went to McDonalds to get food to go. While we were getting gas Jada came over and hugged me. I was still a little teary.

She said, *"Irene, I am glad to be your sister now. We are family for real and I love you three. You're going to be just fine. God is in control."*

All I could muster up was a nod. Jada informed me that we had at least a twelve or thirteen hour drive ahead of us depending on the traffic. She wanted to get there before midnight because she had to work the next day so we were only stopping to gas up and eat on the fly! I'd never driven that far and especially on the highway that long before. I prayed in my head, "Lord please take the wheel."

Jada pulled alongside me as I pulled away from the gas pump.

She rolled down the window and called to us, *"You ready? Now let's ride!"*

Chapter Seven

Jada was not exaggerating about the drive time. It took us a little over thirteen hours but we finally arrived in Massachusetts a little after eleven p.m. We stopped three times; we timed it to stop once about every four hours. When we stopped for gas, I was able to step out and stretch my legs which was great because they were going numb just sitting for that long period of time.

Massachusetts looked old yet beautiful. The weather forecast was calling for snow. Grace politely informed me that it always snows up here. Of course, it snows in Greensboro from time to time but comparably the weather in North Carolina is nothing like up here. Grace told me that Mr. and Mrs. Yancey both tried to get her to tell them where we were. Mr. Yancey wanted to know so he could have us turned in to North Carolina Social Services and Malcolm to the police. Mrs. Yancey, however, seemed really worried about our safety which I thought was ironic as it turned out because we were living in the midst of an unsafe place with a child predator! But she was not going to find out where we were if I could help it! She would never see us ever again.

I was thankful to God for Grace. She talked to me on the phone off and on the whole drive up to Massachusetts. It has only been thirteen hours but I was really missing Malcolm already. Nothing could take my mind off my husband. Oh how I loved the sound of the word "husband!" I was hoping and praying he would just get released and all of this drama would go away quickly.

Jada was renting a house in this college town of Amherst, Massachusetts. The house was across the street from the University of Massachusetts. I googled some information about the school and I learned that it had about 26,000 students total - grads and undergrads. It was considered one of the top universities in the country. This university was humongous! From just the part we drove around to get to Jada's house, it seemed like it stretched out about 15 or 20 blocks! Even this late at night, I saw many young people going to and fro and buses moving about! It looked really busy up here! It reminded me a little of Duke's campus. I was really hoping to get back in school as soon as I could.

Jada showed us around the inside of her home. It was quite nice and immaculately clean. She had it furnished real nice too. There were three bedrooms, two and a half bathrooms, living room, dining room area, and a huge kitchen. I could only imagine this place must cost a mint every month! I also wondered why Jada had a place so big when she was the only one living here. Jada continued her tour and showed us our bedrooms. Abby and I would share a bedroom that was pretty large and had a queen size bed in it. John's room was a little smaller with a full size bed. John was so glad that he would be in a room by himself again. He had already scoped out the fact that both of our rooms had flat screen televisions with cable boxes in them. He was so excited. I told him that he had to be neat and keep his room just like he saw it at that moment. I also reminded him that he was to keep his body clean! He was a teenager with teenage growth issues and I sometimes had to remind him to wash! Ewwww! Boys!

Abby and I were sharing a bedroom. We both needed each other right now. I couldn't imagine how traumatic it was for her with that nasty Mr. Yancey bothering her. I don't how Grace went through that horror for all those years. I thank God she had some kind of sanity left. She made the ride to Massachusetts bearable with her corny jokes that had me rolling in laughter.

Even though it was late, our last food stop was four hours ago. So Jada ordered some pizzas and announced that she was going to bed. She had to be back to work early the next morning. She told me that we would talk more when she got home from work tomorrow afternoon. I could tell Jada was exhausted by her facial expression. I felt like Jada looked! My shoulders were throbbing and my legs and back hurt from sitting so long. Man, how I could use a back rub from Malcolm's strong hands. He was really good at those. My mind was racing. I couldn't stop thinking about Malcolm.

The pizza didn't take long to arrive. John, Abby, and I quickly devoured the large slices and took our clothes up to our rooms to shower and go to bed. I made sure the pizza box was broken down and washed the glasses that we used. It was well past 1 a.m. by the time I finished. As I was leaving the kitchen my cell phone rang. Before I even looked to see who it was, I picked up wishing and hoping it was Malcolm! It was wishful thinking though because it was Grace calling.

"You still up, girl?" she asked as if she forgot what time we arrived.

"Yeah, we just finished eating some pizza so I was cleaning up the kitchen and was about to head to bed. What's up?"

"Girl, Mrs. Yancey wants to talk to you really bad."

"What could she possibly want after all the crap with her sadistic husband? Haven't they done enough?"

"I know Rene." Grace called me Rene occasionally when she was in deep thought about things. *"She wants to know where to send all your birth certificates, shot records, and all your other important documents. She said she was asking me because she knew with everything that had happened that we were not coming back there."*

I sighed, *"that's just like Mrs. Yancey to think of stuff like this because I didn't! I had actually gotten comfortable not having to do those kinds of things anymore because we had the Yancey's. Please let her know that I will call her and give her permission to give you all our documents. Because of Mr. Yancy, Mrs. Yancey is not going to know where we are. It's a shame too because I genuinely loved Mrs. Yancey."*

"I hear you but I feel like she is just as responsible because she knows what he's doing and she is letting him get away with it. But you still need her. She has to go to Social Services and let them know that she is turning Abby and John into your care because you are old enough to care for them. And before Mr. Yancey does something to try to block that and make you all come back."

"Wow, Grace. I didn't know or think about all these things. I'm sure Jada knew because moving here was her idea but we haven't had time to talk about everything in detail yet. Grace, thank you. You have been a big help and a great friend."

"How many times do I have to tell you that you don't have to thank me. You know you guys are my family now too and I got your back!"

"Ok, ok, ok," I said jokingly. *"I won't forget it again. Good night Grace!"*

"Goodnight Rene. Talk at you later!"

I hung up the phone and treaded up the stairs to take my shower. By the time I finally got in the bed with Abby she was already asleep. She rolled over into my arms and I held her just like my mother used to hold me when I was Abby's age. It seemed like I could hear my mother in my head saying, "you, your brother and your sister will be ok." I so wanted Malcolm to be ok too! My mind was still racing which provoked the tears that started running down my cheeks. Just like when my mother was sick, I knew I had to keep myself together for my John and Abby. Now, I had to keep myself together for me and for Malcolm as well. I started praying and eventually my mind stopped racing and I was able to fall asleep.

And oh what a glorious sleep it was. Abby and I slept until 3 p.m. That drive wore the three of us out! My bottom was hurting from sitting, driving in that same position in my car for hours. My shoulders were hurting too!

John was up early. I was barely up and John was milling around.

"Irene, there's a playground across the street with a basketball court. Can I go outside?"

"John, I don't think that's a good idea. We just got here and we don't know a soul here! Besides, it's freezing cold outside. Calm down! You'll get a chance to explore once we become acclimated with the neighborhood."

I knew I needed to get him and Abby into school soon before they lost any significant amount of time. I didn't want them to have to repeat their grades. I knew they both had great grade point averages already. Which reminded me. I pulled out my phone and texted Mrs. Yancy's cell --- Hello Mrs. Yancey. Please give Grace all of our personal documents. Thank you. --- It was straight and to the point. There was no need for anything else.

Jada returned home from work by 5 p.m. She brought in bags and bags of groceries. I had John and Abby help her with the rest of them. Jada gave us all a hug and then she said, *"Irene can you put the groceries away while I go get a shower?"*

"I sure can."

Abby and I started unloading the bags on the kitchen table. John was just standing there looking.

"John, take your butt to your room and watch television 'cause you're just in the way!"

I guess I probably should have been teaching him all this stuff so he would know his way around a kitchen but I figured I still had some time.

Jada finally finished showering and was back in the kitchen in less than thirty minutes. To have worked all day with not a full night's sleep, she was very upbeat! It really seemed like she was glad to have us over. We were in the kitchen laughing and cutting up as Jada started making some chicken stir-fry with white rice. Man, was I relieved. It looked like she had some real skills in the kitchen!

"Jada, your home is beautiful."

"Awe, thank you," she said excitedly. Then she started talking about Malcolm.

"I knew eventually you and Malcolm would get married! Malcom told me that he was going to propose to you the day he got drafted to the NFL. Pro scouts were always at his games."

I was paying attention to what she was saying but the flavor from the food was a huge distraction. I couldn't help but interject.

"Wow Jada, this food is the bomb!"

Jada's cooking was definitely steps above the food Mrs. Yancey had been making! I had actually begun losing a little weight because I wasn't eating a lot and neither was Abby! Abby said the food at school for lunch tasted better than Mrs. Yancey's! Of course, John ate anything that crossed his path. God bless his soul!

We finished eating and Jada asked me to come sit with her in the living-room. Abby cleaned up the kitchen and John watched.

Jada and I sat down and talked for about two hours in her beautiful living-room while Abby and John watched television in the den. Jada laid down the basic rules about her home.

"I know you guys have been through a lot, however, I'm used to living a certain kind of way so in order for this to be a mutually beneficial situation. Most importantly I need you guys to keep the house clean. I don't live in a mess. No one goes in my bedroom. It is completely off limits."

That was understandable. We had to adjust to that at the Yancey's home. Our house was so tiny we were used to being all over the place. Because my mother was sick, her room was my room. I was always there taking care of her.

Jada continued.

"I don't want any dishes left in the sink. And I especially don't want anybody in the house because you guys don't know anyone."

"I agree to abide by the rules and I will convey them to John and Abby. I'm just so thankful that you have opened your home to us. Is it possible I can have the address to give to Grace so that she could mail our records?"

"We're family now Irene and we're going to get through this together. I'm absolutely fine with you giving the address to Grace. Oh...," Jada trailed off, reached for her purse, and pulled out a key from her bag. *"Here is your house key. I'd prefer if you guys could come in through the side entrance instead of the living-room front door. And take off our shoes when you come in and leave them at the door. I don't want to mess up the hardwood floors. But I know you're anxious about Malcolm. I talked to him today and he is doing fine in spite of the circumstances."*

She was right. I was waiting for him to tell me how everything went when he turned himself in. Jada was still talking.

"I gave Pastor Murphy $100.00 to put on Malcolm's account for a phone card so he could call you. You should be expecting him to call around 9:30 p.m. tonight."

I was so excited and Jada could tell I was relieved. I was immediately anxious and I couldn't wait for 9:30 to come.

"Tomorrow I'll show you the school that Abby and John will be attending once all of your paperwork arrives."

"I'd really like that. Everything happened so fast the night of our departure that it never crossed my mind to grab those things when we left."

"We'll go to the Social Services Department so you can apply for Welfare and Food Stamps since you don't have a job. I know you'll qualify for both resources with no problems because Massachusetts is a CommonWealth state and it won't be difficult at all for you to obtain any services you will need. I also feel strongly that you get Abby some counseling after what she had been through."

I was definitely in agreement with that. I felt Abby was strong but she needed someone besides me to talk to. Heck, it probably wouldn't be bad if we all had counseling given the fact that we had all been affected by the events that have happened after my mother's death up until now.

"Oh, how safe is the neighborhood?" I remembered to ask. *"John wants to go to the basketball court across the street."*

"Oh yeah! It's pretty safe. This neighborhood is still very much connected to the University Jada said sure because the University of Massachusetts was right up the street! John just needs to be careful not to bring anyone here. You know how they are. We're right across the street and they'll want to use the bathroom or they'll want something to drink. You guys don't know anyone and I don't want to risk you being taken advantage of. But as you can see, I stocked up so there is plenty of food in the house so you guys can feel free to help yourselves. Irene, can you cook?

I laughed and said, *"a little! My mother taught me a lot, but I didn't get a chance to practice much at the Yancey's! Mrs. Yancey always cooked. But I pitched in as much as I could because she was such a horrible cook."*

"Well my sister, you are here now so cook! You can have dinner ready for me when I get home!"

"No problem!"

Jada stood up and stretched. *"I'm going to bed because I'm going to work early."*

I stood up too and Jada gave me a hug.

"Goodnight 'lil sister. I will see you tomorrow afternoon."

"Ok, Good night."

It was weird hearing someone refer to me as a little sister. Abby had always been the little sister. Jada went straight to her room and went to bed. I was so happy. I thought to myself, "oh my God, this chick is wonderful!" Now I know why Malcolm is the way he is; level headed, polite, and knowledgeable.

I went to the kitchen to check and see if I had to tidy up behind Abby. But I didn't. She had done a wonderful job. I went and got her and John out of the den and told them both to go up to the bedrooms and watch T.V. It was about 8:50 p.m. at that point and Jada said Malcolm was calling at 9:30pm. My heart was pounding. I couldn't wait to talk to him.

I glanced down at my phone and saw that Grace texted me --- MRS. YANCEY DON'T WANT TO GIVE ME YOUR RECORDS!☹ --- This! I picked the phone and dialed Grace's number.

In typical Grace fashion, she was already laughing when she answered the phone.

"I knew you were going to call! Can you believe Irene Mrs. Yancey mean- mugged me and said she wasn't going to give me anything! I just left and came home. I was not about to go there with her."

"I appreciate you trying, Grace. Let me see if I can reach her now. I will call you in the morning. Malcolm is calling soon so I can't stay on."

"Dang girl. I haven't gotten to talk to you all day! But ok. Later chicka! I love you."

"Good night Grace. I love you too."

It was just nine o'clock. I knew that Mr. Yancey didn't get home most times until 10 or 11 p. m. I was hoping he was not home. I dialed the numbers and the phone rang four times. I was getting ready to hang up when Mrs. Yancey answered.

"Hello sweetheart. I'm so glad you called."

"Hey Mrs. Yancey. I can't talk long. Could you please give Grace the stuff I texted you?"

Mrs. Yancey didn't answer the question. Instead she asked, "Are you all ok?"

"We are fine Mrs. Yancey. I'm sorry things popped off the way they did but you should have protected us from Mr. Yancey. You knew he had a problem and you let us move in with a false sense of security thinking everything would be alright. You owe us better than that. You owe my mother better than that. You p…"

Before I could finish my sentence she interrupted.

"Ok, Irene. I will give them to that child in the morning!"

"Thank you. Goodnight Mrs. Yancey. "

I hung up before she could say something else! Wow, she called Grace "that child." She got a lot of nerve! I didn't know why she was so ill. I texted Grace immediately with the update.

---MRS. YANCEY ANSRD MY CLL. U CN PICK UP OUR STUFF IN THE MORN. YOU SHUDNT HVE ANY PROBS. ---

Grace replied. ---😄 OK SIS. TELL MALCOLM I SAID HELLO. ---

My cell rang at exactly 9:28 p.m. It was Malcolm! I hurried into the living room because I didn't want Abby to hear my conversation. I couldn't help but start crying immediately.

"It's alright Irene. Calm down."

I felt like I was hyper-ventilating.

"I love you and I miss you Malcolm."

"I love and miss you too baby."

"What happened Malcolm? How long do you think you're going to be locked up?"

"It doesn't look good. With the trumped up charges Mr. Yancey is accusing me of, I'm looking at five to seven years!"

"What!" I couldn't believe it. *"Malcolm, two to four years is a long time!"*

"Mr. Yancey is a powerful black man in Greensboro and in North Carolina. Everybody believes his story. I've got a garbage Public Defender representing me. It seems like he's on the Prosecuting Attorney's payroll."

I was sobbing as quietly as I could.

"Is there anything I can do?"

"Just take care of John, Abby, and yourself and wait for me. Go to church with Jada and get involved there. Just keep praying and believing in Jesus. He will come through!"

Wow! Malcolm felt like prayer was going to change things. He had a whole lot of faith and at that moment I had none!

"I have my pre-trial arraignment in the morning. So I'm going to try to get some sleep and I'm not trying to use up all my minutes!"

"Alright Malcolm. I love you!"

"I love you too Irene."

And just like that he was gone. I was pissed! At that moment I felt like buying a gun, going back to North Carolina, and blowing Mr. Yancey's 's penis off myself! I went straight to the bathroom to take my shower. I didn't feel like talking to anybody after Malcolm's news. I got in the bed and cried myself to sleep. I was just glad that Abby had already fallen asleep. I didn't want her to hear or see me crying.

I woke up twice with nightmares about Malcolm being locked up in that cold cell. All I could do was think about the worst that could happen to him. I knew I had to get my mind right before I lost it!

Chapter Eight

Malcolm called me every other night. He stayed in jail for months before his trial because we didn't have money or anything to put up for collateral as bail. It didn't matter if we had though, he didn't want us to do that anyway. He was very adamant about the amount of help he would accept... none! He said no Go Fund Me accounts and no fundraising. He wouldn't even let Coach pay for a good attorney. He said he and the Lord would be alright with the public defendant. He also wouldn't let us come down for the trial. He didn't want us to risk being seen by the Yancey's or Social Services. So Jada and Grace went; Jada more so for Malcolm and Grace for me. Grace had a way of converting information spot on and you didn't have to ask her too many questions. She basically told you everything you needed to know.

Malcolm was officially charged with assault and battery and larceny. His attorney did his best to present him as a model citizen. Afterall, he was! He was an upstanding citizen and had a promising future but Mr. Yancey's clout got him sentenced to five years and four months in prison. We were all devastated. I couldn't believe it. I thought we had experienced the worst but here it was again staring us right in the face. I couldn't understand how this was happening but Mr. Yancey made sure he made an example of Malcolm. The maximum sentence for even a first assault and battery offense was only two years. Five years. The words just kept echoing in my mind. Five years. Five years. Five years. Five years was a long time. How were we supposed to live without him for that long? I felt like I was going to have a nervous breakdown or something for sure. But Jada wouldn't hear of it. She already seemed to have a plan to get us all through it.

Jada got to work immediately. She made sure I signed up for every type of assistance available. With the help of Social Services and Section Eight Housing, it didn't take long for me to acquire my own home. Even though we no longer lived with Jada, I knew she was preparing us to be ready in our own home when Malcolm did come home. Massachusetts was also a Commonwealth State which made it a lot easier to get on your feet.

We got a nice three bedroom house in Amherst not too far from Jada. As soon as I got the keys to our new place, Grace headed to Massachusetts. She completely relocated to live with us and help out while I worked and went to school. Grace received a fat check every month from Social Security Disability to do nothing, so her moving in with us was a bonus. Of course, the chick was clean as well and we got along real good. Abby and John adored her too. She was the other Aunt they never had. Someone else who loved them and wanted nothing else but the best for them. Abby and John had transitioned well from North Carolina and were doing great in school. Malcolm, on the other hand, was not well with the idea of Grace moving to Massachusetts to live with us at first. But in light of everything we'd all been through, I asked him to give Grace a chance. As much as I loved Jada, she and I didn't have the relationship Grace and I had and with Malcolm being gone from our lives for so long, I needed someone on my level who would be with me through that time. Malcolm wasn't feeling it but I told him if she didn't work out, I would send her back to North Carolina.

While we were setting up house, Malcolm was doing his time one day at a time. I had to admit, everytime we spoke he was always positive and optimistic. He was determined to not allow his having to do time get the best of him. He got busy! He started a ministry in prison. They had bible class on Wednesday evenings and a Sunday morning worship service. Malcolm said the ministry was growing by leaps and bounds. He spoke about it with so much excitement that I wished I could hear him preach or teach or whatever he was doing. He told me that a preacher from High Point, North Carolina whose name was Pastor Nehemiah Washington, came to the prison on Sunday evenings to preach the Word of God to the inmates. He said this Pastor was real good and described him as real charismatic. He even said that the inmates were singing and dancing in the Holy Spirit! Malcolm said there were at least two hundred inmates who showed up for the Sunday morning and Sunday evening services. I believe Malcolm will become an ordained minister once he gets out.

As for me, I started working for the welfare Department of Social Services. I must say it was a job I hated, but it was a job! It did allow me the flexibility to attend school four days a week which was a huge blessing! I had two scheduled days on campus and two days online. With everything going on, I knew I couldn't abandon my mother's hopes and dreams of being the first in my family to graduate from college.

It had been extremely challenging adjusting to our new lives and without Malcolm. We'd been joined at the hip for so long,

I never imagined that I would ever have to live without him. Men hit on me constantly and having my first sexual experience on my honeymoon night lit a fire in me that I'd been trying to squelch ever since. I had to be the horniest chick in Massachusetts! Regardless of how I feel though, I was committed to waiting on my man. I was staying focused and I, myself, hoped to graduate from college in the next two and a half years. I had to admit that moving to Massachusetts was a great idea. Even though it was very different from Greensboro, we took to it quickly and we loved it.

John and Abby were doing well. John made the high school basketball team and he was pretty good! His coaches were really big on him. Physically, he shot up to a six foot five inch frame just like our father, Mr. Nathan, and the little girls were always blowing up his cell phone everyday. I was always telling him that he better not be trying to have sex with these silly little girls. With everything else we've had to deal with, we didn't need any teenage pregnancies around our home. I knew he was listening and probably somewhat embarrassed by the conversation so he always laughed and then said he was not doing anything. Let's just say for all of our sakes, I hoped he wasn't.

Abby was doing well also. I was so proud of her. She was growing into a wonderful young lady. Abby aspired to be class president and valedictorian of her high school senior class and her current GPA had her on track to possibly be awarded a full scholarship to the University of Massachusetts. That was where she wanted to attend. In our transition to Massachusetts and from Jada's house to our own, Abby managed to gain a boyfriend. He was Jewish and Caucasian. I'm not judging her choice, I'm just saying!

As soon as we got settled, I got some help for Abby with counseling and she faithfully attended her sessions. She knew that what Mr. Yancey did to her was not her fault. She understood that Mr. Yancey was simply a predator who needed help. Overall and considering the circumstances, I was glad that Abby was doing just fine.

Mrs. Yancey hadn't given up on us even though I wouldn't have blamed her if she did. She kept in touch with Grace because she knew Grace knew where we were. I still wasn't about to let Mrs. Yancey know where we lived. I was afraid she'd show up at our door and try to take John and Abby from me. She did convince Grace to allow her to send her money for us without her husband knowing. She always sent it with her credit card to Grace through Western Union. I felt sorry for her because she was a sweetheart. It just baffled me that she covered for the predator and rapist who was her husband. I didn't understand how she could live in that silence knowing Mr. Yancey was a sick man.

The money Mrs. Yancey wired to us every month was a huge blessing. It was usually three hundred dollars. I did call her on her birthday a couple of months ago. We both cried and I told her I loved her. I explained to her that I appreciated all that she has done for us. I promised her that Abby and John were doing great and that I would send a picture of us soon. It was time we took family pictures so I could also send Malcolm some. He sent us pictures of himself inside. He had gotten so big from lifting weights. Oooh wee! I needed to stop before I got myself all worked up! Jesus!

Grace really loved Amhurst as well. It had a large Lesbian community and she seems to fit right in. Malcolm said that Lesbianism was a sinful act! I never told Grace how he felt and what he believed. He always asked if she had ever tried to push up on me since she'd been living with us and thankfully I could always say no! Grace knew the deal and she had honestly become my best friend and another Aunt for John and Abby. She had her friends, but she never entertained at our home. When she stayed out, it was usually never more than one night. The chick could cook and she loved to cook. She was always watching the Food Network and knitting something. She was an old soul. Grace was a true blessing to our household.

Grace said moving to Massachusetts was meant to be. Her parents had retired and moved to Alabama. Grace wasn't close to her parents at all even though she was an only child. Grace loved Amhurst because there was 24-hour transportation on the bus lines unlike in North Carolina where everything stopped running at 9 p.m. It should not have been surprising though. Afterall, this was a major college town. Grace said that her parents didn't agree with her becoming a lesbian and had a problem with the LGBTQ Community altogether. Since Grace moved in, she shared a lot with me about the years Mr. Yancey molested and raped her. He sodomized her and made her have sex with him and other women. As Grace got older, Mr. Yancey bought her any and everything she wanted. I'm sure he thought that was supposed to make up for what he was putting her through. It began to be more than she could handle and eventually she became an alcoholic and got three DWI's. Grace said she drank because she hated herself. She sounded so free when she spoke of the moment she told Mr. Yancey they wouldn't be having sex anymore. She said he was pissed and he was not accepting of her decision and started acting like a teenage stalker. He couldn't understand why she didn't want to be with him sexually anymore. Grace told him she was a Lesbian and he laughed! The nerve of that piece of crap predatory jerk to laugh! I should have known something was up the time that punk tried to feel me up while hugging me after he gave me the keys to my car. I can't stand him. I asked Grace how she felt being around Mrs. Yancey all those years. She immediately burst into tears because one day she came to the realization that she was wrong. Mrs. Yancey didn't deserve any of what she was living.

Every week I got a money order to mail to Malcolm. I sent him $25.00 a week. I wanted to send more but he always insisted that $25.00 a week was enough. He said that $25.00 allowed him to eat pretty well and feed some of his inmate friends who don't get anything from their families. That's just like my husband to think of others. Jada still sent him calling card numbers so he could call us often. Grace commented that she could always see the excitement on my face when it was time to talk to him. She teased me and when she did I always told her to mind her business and we'd both have a good laugh.

I usually took a shower so I could relax in bed when Malcolm called. I went to John's room to make sure he had completed his school assignments. I stayed in after him to keep his grades up. Colleges were writing concerning him already. He was in the tenth grade and he'd started playing varsity basketball. Oh how Malcolm wished he was home to see John play! John was averaging eighteen points a game. I didn't understand all the stats yet but Malcolm said if he was averaging eighteen points in the tenth grade, he was already a beast. Alright!

I told John to clean up his room because it was a mess and to hang up the phone with the little girls. John thought he was a little player now. Oh, don't worry, he will be talking to Malcolm. John knew Malcolm did not play when it came to his school work. Malcolm stayed on John to do his best in school. Malcolm told him to chill when it came to the fast little girls. Malcolm always let me know that it took two to tango and that John wasn't innocent. It was not just the fast little girls.

I peeked into my room to see that Abby was fast asleep. She didn't play when it came to her sleep. I never had to check to see if Abby had done her homework. That little chick was on point.

My sister was so gorgeous and I was so proud of her. Who would have thought that with all we have been through that Abby would excel the way she had. She had the highest GPA in her class. She had already received a full scholarship to the University of Massachusetts. Abby said she wanted to become a surgeon. I believed her! She was so driven. I knew my Mother was rejoicing in heaven. I never understood, though, what she saw in her curly haired Jewish boyfriend. His parents were wealthy and he was very smart too. The little brat was rotten to the core when it came to respecting his parents. The way he talked to them was crazy! One day I told him that God wasn't pleased with the way he was carrying on. It was terrible. I knew he didn't talk to Abby like that though. Abby would not have tolerated it. He looked at me and apologized. The boy looked a little scared at that moment too. In my head I was like, *"Good!"* He needed to check his spoiled, privileged self. I didn't want to scare him too much though. I wasn't alone. Abby got on him as well. The little brat apologized and said that it would not happen again. I told him he needed to cherish his blessed parents. I reminded him that Abby, John, and I lost our mother at a young age and that we would give anything to have her back. I also explained to him that it was not easy raising two younger siblings without our parents.

I could never remember Abby's boyfriend's name. It was Josh; short for Joshua. He said that I should write a memoir about what my family had been through. Abby heard him and agreed that I should tell our story. I was surprised I never thought about our story being worthy to be put in a book. I told them that I would seriously consider it. I had to always contemplate exposing us until we got to the place where no one could hurt us or take John and Abby away from me.

Chapter Nine

Malcolm called at 9:50 p.m. on the dot.

"Hey wifey!" He always sounded excited to talk to me.

"Hello husband," I giddily replied. *"How are you making out this week?"*

"I'm doing good baby, real good." He paused. *"Guess what?*

"What baby?" I asked curiously.

"Someone put $500.00 on my account."

"Wow Malcolm, that's great?"

I knew how he felt about having too much money on his books. But then my mind started racing! I was wondering if it was some chick I didn't know about. I quickly erased the thought of another woman off my mind. I quickly said to myself, "The devil is a liar"! I heard Malcom use that phrase all the time so I figured it worked. I also heard the Pastor at the church we attended say it often. I didn't want to go down this negative street in my mind. I believe my husband was honest enough to tell me if any woman sent him anything! Only me and Jada were allowed. Case closed! I had to convince myself not to let the thought of another woman play with my mind!

"Well I guess it has to be because whoever it was put cash and they wanted to remain anonymous."

"Well Jesus is looking out for you that's for sure."

That was the only explanation I could come up with. I was thinking about who would give Malcolm that kind of money in prison? Malcolm and I had talks about me and negative thoughts many times over the last few months. Trust me, tonight was one of those moments.

"Who do you think it might have been?" I asked.

I was still trying not to let it bother me, but it was.

"I haven't the slightest idea. The money came with a note thanking me for ministering to the inmates and for showing them love and compassion."

"Aww, that is sweet honey."

"I believe the $500 came from Pastor Nehemiah and his church."

"Really!"

Malcolm explained, "Pastor Nehemiah is not allowed to give money to an inmate being that he is the Prison Chaplain. Chaplain's are considered employees. Employees cannot give an inmate anything. I know one thing. I'm not going to keep wondering about it. I am going to tell the Lord thank you!"

Then he said, "Irene, you have no reason to worry because I am in love with you!"

I guess he could tell the money thing was bothering me.

He continued, "So you don't have to send me $25.00 a week for a while. I do, however, need a new pair of sneakers."

"Ok. What kind?"

"Something inexpensive. Remember I told you that high end sneakers can cause a huge fight inside prison. A lot of inmates do not receive anything from their family and friends. It's sad. Some of the inmates have not heard from their family and friends in years. This

$500.00 will be great for me to help some of the inmates. I'll have to bless them secretly without them finding out where the blessings came from, though. If they think you've got money, they will beg and harass me for stuff."

"That is so nice of you to think of others inside, Malcom."

I tried to sound happy but I don't think it was convincing because I was still smoking about who sent him that kind of money!

Before we knew it, Malcolm's talk time was over. Before he hung up, he prayed and said, *"always remember Irene, I'm in love with you."*

I was blushing so hard you could probably see two plum patches on the cheeks of my dark skin.

"Goodnight Malcolm. I love you," I said lovingly.

I had to get myself together for bed because I had a long day ahead with work and John's basketball game after school. Abby, Grace, and I usually went to all of John's games. He would have had a fit if we didn't attend. I just thank God he was keeping his grades up. I wanted him to receive a full-ride scholarship to a good university just like his sister and I did.

I was starting to wind down for sleep when my mind started to ponder what it would be like if my mother was still alive. I wondered, under the circumstances, if she would be proud of us. I know she would have loved to have Malcolm as a son-in-law. I also wondered if she would have tried to find our trifling father! The thought of that sorry man gets on my nerves. Mr. Yancey and Mr. Nathan were the worst two men ever in my short life! But I had to let it go. I knew I'd never get to sleep with that on my mind.

When I finally managed to drift off to sleep, I heard Grace in the living-room talking very loudly on the phone. It was well after midnight. As she got closer to the hallway, I noticed her speech was somewhat slurred like she might have been a little intoxicated. She went back to her room and closed her door. It really sounded like she stumbled a lil too! I got up out of the bed and went to her bedroom door. I knocked lightly and whispered, *"Grace, you are talking too loud!"* She opened the door slightly.

When she looked up at me and said, *"I'm so sorry Irene."*

I could see the tears running down her cheeks. Now that we were face to face, I could also tell that Grace was drunk! I was instantly upset and concerned at the same time. Grace didn't need to be drinking. She was a recovering alcoholic! I deliberately stayed up until Grace got off the phone.

"What's going on Grace?" I asked as I peered into the doorway of her room.

She was acting very weird, *"what do you mean Irene?"*

"Grace, don't play with me," I yelled. *"You are drunk!"*

She started crying again.

"I'm sorry Irene. My girlfriend broke up with me."

Even though I was angry, the fact was she was drunk and I immediately felt bad for the chick. What in the world could I say to her? At that moment I realized that I didn't know how to console my friend. I'd never been through a relationship break-up myself so I couldn't empathize with her at all. I silently selfishly thanked God!

I counted to ten in my head and then I moved beside Grace and gave her a hug. Ooh wee! She was torn up tipsy and she reeked of alcohol!

"I'm so sorry for you Grace. I'm sorry for how you are feeling right now at this very moment."

That was all I had.

"I'm going to the kitchen to make some coffee. You want some?"

On the way to the kitchen I started asking God, *"Lord, what am I supposed to say to Grace right now that would make some kind of a difference?"*

I finished making the coffee and took a cup of it back to Grace. When I got back to the room, I realized this chick was knocked out sleep just that fast! I went over to her to check to see if she was asleep or dead. Thank God, she was breathing!

I took the coffee back to the kitchen, went back to my room, and got back in my bed. By now, Abby was snoring pretty loud. I nudged her and told her to turn over while laughing at her quietly. Malcolm had me in the habit of praying before I laid down for the night as well as praying when I arose the next morning. At that moment, I got on my knees and thanked God for my family. I thanked God in advance for an early release for my husband. I had asked Abby and John to also pray that prayer too! I knew Malcolm's sister Jada was constantly praying that same prayer and we were altogether trusting and believing God for the same thing. Lastly, I thanked God for all our safety including Grace and Mrs. Yancey and then I drifted off to sleep.

At 6:30 a.m. and I woke up to the smell of what I thought was turkey bacon, eggs, and grits. Grace was usually up this early with breakfast ready for us. As I entered the kitchen I could see Abby was already dressed for school and eating. John was still in the bathroom, of course.

"Good morning," Abby spoke cheerfully.

"Good morning Shug," I sang back. Grace was washing dishes in the sink trying not to make eye contact with me.

"Irene," Abby fired. *"I want to go to my Senior Prom. Can you take me to look for a dress?"*

"Abby, how awesome! When is the prom?" I asked excitedly.

Abby replied, *"It's at the end of May."*

"Child, we have a few months but sure we can look for something. We will get you straight. Do you know what color scheme you want to wear?"

"I think I want to wear an African gown or dress!"

Her response definitely threw my mind for a loop! I wasn't ready. Why in the world did this child want to wear some African garb to a prom with a Jewish white boy? I couldn't figure this one out for the world.

I fixed my plate and sat down to eat. John was just coming out to eat as well. He was so greedy! Still curious, I called Abby back into the kitchen.

"Are you planning on going to the prom with Josh?" I could hear Grace laughing in the background.

"Uh, yes!" Abby replied, sounding slightly annoyed.

"Does he know what you want to wear to the prom?"

"Yes Irene. Josh loves African prints. He actually loves the African jungles. He wants to visit Africa when he graduates high school."

"That's impressive," I was very surprised! I was so curious about what this Jewish white boy was going to wear with Abby's African print but I figured I better leave it alone. Abby had finished her breakfast and headed out for school.

I left John at the table and headed to Grace's room. I knocked on the door.

"Grace, can I come in?"

"Sure."

I went into Grace's room and moved the chair from her desk.

"Are you alright?" I asked. Grace started crying again. All I could think was oh my God!

"Rene, I am so in love with her."

"I'm so sorry Grace. Why did she break up with you?"

"I'm so embarrassed Rene. She caught me cheating with another girl."

"Oh my God Grace! Why are you cheating?" Before she could answer I said, "I'm sorry girl, you don't have to answer that." Here I was getting another mind-blower and this early in the morning! "This is what you're going to do. You are going to stop drinking immediately and you are going to get up and find you some AA meetings. I am not playing with your alcoholism Grace. You know Abby, John, and I lived through my mother's addition and I refuse to do it again. I love you Grace but I cannot allow any of this nonsense. If you are going to continue to stay with us, this has to happen right now."

Grace nodded that she understood. She had become such a vital part of our family and it hurt me so much to see her like this.

"I know you are hurting and I just want you to know that I do care how you are feeling and I will be praying for you." As soon as I had uttered the words it seemed like God was telling me to pray with Grace right then. So I did! I went and grabbed Grace's hands and began to petition to the Lord on her behalf. I asked God through His son Jesus Christ to stop Grace's heart from hurting and to make her alcohol addiction cease! She was really sobbing at that point. I hugged her again and told her that she would be alright. Then I walked out of her room to get myself ready for work.

The house seemed unusually quiet with Abby and John already gone for school. When I came out of my room to leave for work, Grace was in the kitchen cleaning up our mess from breakfast. As I headed out the door, I yelled to Grace, "see ya later!"

Grace yelled back, "thank you Irene."

"You're welcome Grace and you are worth it. Don't forget John has a game this afternoon at four."

"Ok, I will be ready," she said, already starting to sound like her old self again.

I was so intrigued that God had compelled me to pray for Grace. Malcolm would probably think I was joking if I told him about me praying for Grace but I actually couldn't wait to tell him! I think I will keep the part about her being drunk to myself though.

Chapter Ten

As I worked through my day, all I could think about was Grace. I was worried that her alcohol problem would increase especially with her dealing with the breakup of her relationship. I had never seen this chick so distraught the whole three years we'd been friends. I was also going back and forth in my head trying to decide whether or not I should tell Malcolm. I didn't even want to think about what he might say but I also didn't want Grace drinking around Abby and John. They thought very highly of Grace and I knew this would hurt them.

Finally it was time for my lunch break and I got up and went for a walk just outside of my job. Boy did I really hate this job but it was Malcolm's voice ringing in my head with the scripture from the bible saying, *"despise not small beginnings."* Malcolm always told me to stay humble. He would back that up by also saying God was seeing if he could trust me with all I had before my increase arrived. I felt like I was doing all I could to hold the fabric of our little family together and succeed in making this work. Malcolm always ends our conversation by telling me, *"baby, you are doing a phenomenal job!"*

My thirty minute lunch break was just about over when I decided to call home and check on Grace. I wanted to know if she found an AA meeting to attend. I didn't want her sitting around in guilt and shame all day. I also wanted her to start attending church on Sundays. Grace needed to get involved with other great people. Malcolm asked me from time to time if Grace attended church with us? I always said, *"No, Grace didn't go."* I always had to remind Malcolm that Grace didn't believe in God! Of course, Malcolm would blare over the phone, *"how could she not believe in our precious Jesus?"* Then he would carry on and on saying that God had been good to Grace too and she needed to give Him a real chance to prove that He was real. Anyway, the phone just rang and I didn't get an answer when I called, which was strange. Grace always answered the phone when I called. I immediately began to worry. I felt like taking the rest of the day off from work but I quickly shrugged off that thought. I wanted to be able to trust God first and also trust Grace.

My thoughts began to wander off in memory of my mother's addiction. She was hooked on crack and other stuff for so many years. It broke my heart to even think about those crazy times! She stayed high all day and all night everyday of the week. There were so many nights Abby and I had to put her in the tub because the terrible stench of vomit and days of not bathing became too much for us to bear! She literally smelled of any and everything she'd been around; marijuana, cigarettes, and that insane crack cocaine smell when mixed with tequila, vodka, beer, and vomit! It was gross! Under the influence of all that stuff, mom didn't care! After she sobered up, she would thank us for cleaning her up. I knew, if nothing else, she felt better afterwards.

When she got cleaned up is when she talked to me the most. It always seemed to be about her health problems though. She was doing too much to her body. She would always ask Abby if she wanted to cook a meal together. With the food stamps she used to purchase the food, she never knew if we had the right ingredients or enough ingredients to make the meal turn out like she wanted. I thank God my mother taught me how to shop and keep food in the house. We fed a lot of junkies and alcoholics back then too. Malcolm always said that God was going to heal and deliver one of those addicted persons and they were going to come and thank us for what we had done! My response was always, *"they can stay sober but keep it moving!"* I really didn't want to see anybody from that crazy season in our lives. Abby and John didn't need to see them either. I was just glad that I never got into drinking booze or using drugs for that matter.

Those old memories of my beloved late mother were heart wrenching. They were so visual that they seemed to be seared in my head. I was also still very much pissed off that my lousy-good-for-nothing father, Mr. Nathan, impregnated my mother with the three of us, introduced my mother to those horrible drugs, left my mother with a horrible habit, then got clean and completely abandoned us. He was a jerk and a coward in my book.

I needed to quickly get my head together because I was still at work. I didn't want my co-workers seeing me shed a tear. None of them knew anything about my past life. They knew nothing about Malcolm being in prison and I dared not share any of those details with them because my story would have spread around that workplace like diarrhea in a wetsuit. I already hated working there. Social Services/welfare was hard enough. Although I was grateful for a job, they didn't pay nearly enough.

Just then I just got a text. It was Grace.

SORRY 4 NOT ANSRG UR CALL. FOUND AA MTG N. HAMPTON NXT 2 SMITH COLLEGE.

My heart leaped with joy because she took my advice and found a meeting at Smith College in North Hampton Massachusetts. Smith College was also known for being a Lesbian University because it was where a lot of the lesbian community attended. Northampton was also known for being a Lesbian University. I heard there were really nice people there but I kept my siblings away as much as possible. It was a tough line to tow. I was trying to keep them from what I felt would be unnecessary distractions in their lives while also trying to teach them not to discriminate against any group of people. I was hoping and praying Grace got back on track and stayed on track.

With less than an hour left of work, my thoughts turned toward John. I was getting excited about his basketball game. Colleges from all over the country were writing, calling, texting, and attending his games. He was considered what we young folks described as a beast at small forward. He was ranked fourth in the country in high school basketball. Malcolm kept me straight with all the basketball lingo. He told me John was considered a very special player because of his natural ability. Surprisingly enough, Abby also said John was really good but you would never get her to say it in earshot of John! Those two were a trip! Malcolm wished he was out of prison so he could help guide John in the right direction. It was not so long ago that pro scouts were watching Malcolm.

With my workday ended, I pulled into my driveway just as my neighbor, Mr. Harlem, was coming out of his back door. He was a handsome man and a real flirt. He was always trying to take me out to which my response was always an emphatic *"No,"* followed by *"not ever happening!"* My response didn't seem to deter Mr. Harlem. He just kept on trying. Unlike Mr. Yancey, though, Mr. Harlem was harmless. He had genuine care and concern for all of us. He always made sure we were alright. Mr. Harlem hit on Grace too but she always told him to go to hell! I guess after Mr. Yancey, Grace didn't take any junk from nor did she kid around with men like Mr. Harlem. I had to often tell Grace to lighten up.

As soon as I got in the house, I was ambushed by Abby and Grace. They were rearing and ready to get to John's game.

"You guys! I have to go to the bathroom!" I yelled as I ran past them.

It didn't take me long and we all filed into the car and headed to the school. Abby told me her homework was completed. She knew that came first. Although, she didn't really need to announce it because I knew she lived for being studious. I knew my mother would have demanded this as well if she were alive. I really missed her but I could feel her pushing me in ways I could not explain. It was almost like she was with me. I vividly remembered the last two years of her life. My mother seemed at peace. She had beaten her addiction and I was so glad. I thought all of our problems would have been solved at that point. She stopped inviting people over; mostly men and mostly disgusting looking, smelly, and disrespectful people who were in and out of our apartment all night. My mother allowed them to sleep in our living room. Abby, John, and I had to stay in our backroom. We barely ate a lot of those days during my mother's addiction because we were too afraid to come out in the kitchen to get food. I secretly cried myself to sleep a lot of those nights. I tried not to let Abby and John see me like that. I thank God that my mother was scared straight though. She got herself together after she caught John playing with her needles and other drug paraphernalia. That was all it took. She had finally hit her rock bottom.

But to have her pass away so suddenly after being clean and sober her last two years alive was devastating to me. It was so surreal. I remember feeling like I was having an out of body experience. I also thanked God for Mrs. Yancey because at times I thought, I myself, was going to die. Even though they didn't like our life when my mother was addicted, I know it hurt Abby and John to lose her as well. I couldn't understand why God took my mother while she was doing good. I might have understood it more if she would have died while she was abusing drugs. Malcolm always told me that we would never understand everything concerning God but that we should have faith in Him anyway. And I did!

Once we got in the gymnasium, I told Abby to go get us some hot dogs and cokes. She and I loved to eat the junk food the high school sold. We would get popcorn and candy apples as well. Grace always looked at us in disgust which we thought was hilarious. She didn't eat like we did. She was actually slowly becoming a vegan. We always got a chuckle over Grace and her weird ways. Abby and I, on the other hand, didn't care nothing about being vegan. I was just rejoicing that Grace didn't seem to be all messed up over the breakup of her and her girlfriend. She was pretty sauced last night but it seemed the AA meeting had done some good.

The game started and John's team was quickly up by eleven points. There were television news cameras all over the gym. John had seven of those eleven points with two dunks that caused the gymnasium to erupt in loud roars and cheers with the little high school cheerleaders doing their thing. John showed me at one of the games we attended last year where the college scouts sat. You couldn't miss them. There were many men with clipboards. My prayer every night was that John graduate high school with a full scholarship when he graduated. I also prayed that Malcolm would be released sooner than later. Taking care of John and Abby made me feel more motherly than before and I felt myself thinking about what it would be like to have a baby with my husband. The thought of it was still a little scary to me. Although I was sure Malcolm and I would probably make a beautiful baby. At that moment I decided to change my speech to that of faith and say one day soon Malcolm and I would have a beautiful child.

My thoughts were short lived as I was distracted by Abby tearing up the snacks! I laughed to myself. Just then I looked up and saw Abby's boyfriend, Josh, coming towards us. It seemed like he was pretty popular because a lot of those young kids were speaking to him on his way over and giving him high fives. Abby slid over and made room for him to sit down.

At a minute and six seconds left in the game, John's team was winning by eighteen points. It was a blow out! I was enjoying watching John play but I couldn't wait for it to be over because I was tired. With everything that was going on with Grace, I didn't get much sleep last night. I was hoping she had her stuff together. Who would've thought this would happen? For two years Grace was so cool. Well, she is still cool. She's my friend. I just truly didn't see this happening.

When the game was finally over, we waited for John to shower and come out of the locker room. I thought we'd be able to leave right away but immediately after John came out of the locker room, he had two interviews with two different local news networks. I wondered why they didn't interview John right after the game? Abby could see I was becoming irritable and she showed me John's so-called girlfriend. She was a cheerleader, of course and she looked Hispanic. She was very cute. I was just hoping John wasn't having sex. Although I thought to myself, when did he have a chance too. He seemed to have his hands full between class, studying, and practice. I knew I would probably need to get Malcolm to have that talk with him again because he was sick of me asking. Watching John talk with the reporters, all I could think about was how much he looked like our father. Even though I hadn't seen the man in years, I distinctly remembered how Mr. Nathan looked. It was extremely nerve wrecking because even though I hated him, I had to admit that he was a very handsome man and we all were pretty good looking too.

When we finally arrived home, our land line was ringing off the hook. It was college coaches, scouts, and AAU reps all calling to talk to John. I knew it was all very exciting for him but I really wanted him to stay focused on his school work. Before I could say anything, John started, *"Irene..."* he said with his voice trailing off.

"What's up superstar?" I teased as I punched him in his arm. But he didn't return my playfulness.

"I need to talk to you about something."

My mind immediately started racing again. With everything I had just been through with Grace the night before, I wasn't sure I had the energy to deal with anything else. Abby had also just shown me John's girlfriend so it could have been anything.

"Ok," I responded, my voice then trailing off.

"I'm struggling in Math."

"That's all?" I didn't mean to say that out loud. *"I'm sorry I meant to say that's not a problem."* He looked at me strangely.

"You told me if I was having problems with anything..." I didn't let him finish.

"Yes, John. You're good. That's an easy fix." Of course my first thought was that Abby could help him, but I knew John would not cooperate with his sister so we will not go there! *"I will get you*

a tutor to come over in the evenings when you don't have practice and we'll get you straight. Don't worry John, I got you."

"*Thanks sis!*" His smile was back and the look of concern was no longer there.

Although I didn't like my job, it afforded me access to lots of resources. The State of Massachusetts offered many services and tutoring for low-income students. It would even be convenient for them. Afterall, our home was only a couple of blocks from the University of Massachusetts. Most of the tutors in our area came from the university. Hopefully John would get some mathematical geek. At any rate, I would be calling John's math teacher tomorrow to find out where John was struggling. I knew he wanted to keep his B average so he could make sure he got that full scholarship. I had to make sure I checked on him like our mother checked on me and my grades. Even those last two years of her life, she didn't play when it came to my grades. I was too scared not to bring home A's! But I didn't want to be that drastic to my siblings. They were my world. With my mother deceased and my father estranged, they were my only blood family. I would die for Abby and John. I loved it when they both told me they loved me. I told my mother all the time that I loved her. She really loved that.

Chapter Eleven

It was a cold Massachusetts morning and I was headed out to work with Malcolm on my mind. This was our night to talk and I was excited just as I always was when it was our night to talk. With everything going on, I still hadn't found time to get Malcolm a pair of sneakers and put them in the mail. I was also still thinking about whoever was sending him money and what their intentions were. All I knew was that it better not be some chick trying to get with Malcolm. I didn't want to complain though. Besides, Malcolm would just tell me to stop overthinking it. Even though we only get fifteen minutes, we get a lot said in that time.

I decided to take my lunch break today to make a quick run to Dick's Sporting Goods. It was just around the corner from the job. They had lots of things I liked for Malcolm including a nice pair of all black Nikes. I was hoping they weren't too fancy because I didn't want anyone trying to beat Malcolm up for his shoes. Then I went to the deli across the street and bought a corn beef sandwich with coleslaw, Reuben sauce, and a dill pickle. That sandwich was crazy good! They put so much meat on my sandwich that I only ever ate half and I always asked for extra bread to take the rest home. John gladly finished it off everytime.

It was two weeks from Christmas and last week, we'd gotten the first real snow. It was only about seven inches but there were a little bit of snow flurries forecasted for today. Even though seven inches was a drop in the bucket compared to how much it usually snowed in Massachusetts, I already didn't want to see any more of that white stuff! I hated driving in the snow and I hated having to pay someone to shovel my steps, driveway, and sidewalk. Trust me, John will be learning how to shovel snow. Malcolm says that I should have had him doing it two years ago. There was hardly ever any snow in my home city of Greensboro in North Carolina. It hardly ever snowed there. I missed home a lot even though my siblings and I were doing great in Massachusetts.

After I got home, showered, and ate dinner I patiently waited for my phone time with Malcolm. Grace teased me. She said I was always like a schoolgirl getting to talk to my boyfriend for the first time. I had to admit that it was always like that when Malcolm called. I wasn't sure if it was the anxiety of making sure I was by that phone when it rang so I wouldn't miss the call. I just knew I loved his voice being the last voice I heard before I got to drift off into an abysmal sleep.

The next morning I woke up happy, refreshed, and glad it was Saturday. That was until my cell phone rang. Who in the world was calling me on a Saturday morning? I glanced over to see if the caller was about to get my voicemail and I saw it was Grace. I thought she told me she was going to a morning AA meeting. I immediately got nervous. Grace usually didn't call me unless there was something wrong.

"Grace?" I answered, trying not to sound worried.

"Rene! Guess what? You'll never guess," Grace almost shrieked.

"Ok, what then?" I said knowing she was bursting at the seams to dish some type of tea!

"I just talked to Mrs. Yancey."

"Let me guess! Mr. Yancey fell off of one of his construction buildings to his death!" I burst into a fit of laughter. "I should be so lucky!"

"Well...." Grace stammered. "Almost but not quite."

"Ok Grace. Spill it!"

"Irene, Mrs Yancey just told me that Mr. Yancey was in the hospital dying from stage four prostate cancer!"

"Oh my goodness! I probably shouldn't have said that awful thing. I mean I've thought worse but you never actually feel good to hear someone is actually dying, do you?" I felt bad not just because Mr. Yancey was dying but because it brought back the sting that I felt when my mother died.

Grace continued. "Mrs. Yancey was pretty messed up!"

"She is messed up? I am pretty thrown back myself! Even though this man did what he did to Abby and Malcolm, I still feel bad for Mrs. Yancey."

I wondered what Mrs. Yancey would do now without Mr. Yancey. From my understanding she had always been a housewife. I didn't think she had put any time into the workforce. Plus Mrs. Yancey was in her early 70's. She volunteered a lot for the homeless shelter and also the Red Cross. When we lived with her, she was faithful with that kind of stuff. That was how she met my Mother and they became very good friends.

"Wow Grace! Poor Mrs. Yancey." I suddenly felt the urge to call her. "Are you on your way home?" I asked.

I didn't know if Grace had other plans for the day. John had a Christmas tournament game in West Springfield later. Even though it was Saturday, neither Grace nor I drove to the real far away games, especially with the snow flurries in the forecast. I'd also promised Abby we'd look for her a gown or dress for her prom. I hadn't said anything to her though. I knew she thought I'd forgotten.

"*Yes!*"

"*Ok girl. We'll talk more about this when you get here!*"

"*Later!*"

"*Later chicka!*"

West Springfield was forty-five minutes from Amherst. Even though we weren't going to be there, we hoped John would win. It had only been a few weeks since I'd gotten him tutoring but it was already paying off. He pulled his grade point back up to a B average. All of that was credit to the tough tutor I arranged for him from the University who didn't take no junk from him! I was so glad she was tough on him and made sure he didn't slack off. Heck, I was scared of her myself!

I got cleaned up and went downstairs to finish wrapping up Malcolm's sneakers to be mailed. I should have had them in the mail weeks ago. Sorry baby! Once I finished up, I sat the sneakers by the door so I'd see them on my way out and remember to put them in the car. I also set a reminder on my cell to mail out Malcolm's sneakers. This was his Christmas present. I hated that this would be another year I had to spend Christmas and the New Year without my sexy husband. I think it was what stopped me from making New Year's resolutions. Most folks didn't honor them anyway. I did need to start exercising though because in the two years I'd been in Massachusetts, I'd put on about ten pounds. I was still shapely though. Men were still always trying to date me but I was not doing that! I did get horny from time to time but I am human. I confessed this to Malcolm and he just laughed at me and told me to pray through it! Malcolm admitted though that he gets horny too. He told me imagine what he has to deal with; a bunch of grown men around him all the time.

He said he hated to hear and see grown men inside the prison masturbating. I told Malcolm that was too much information. I know it's what they have to do to get through it but I thought it was so disgusting.

With nothing else pressing to do, I slid into the chair in the living room and picked up my phone to call Mrs. Yancey. I blocked my number though. I didn't want Mrs. Yancey blowing up my phone like she did Grace. Grace said Mrs. Yancey always called her asking about us.

"Hello." She sounded so frail.

"Hello, Mrs. Yancey, " I began.

"Irene, is that you?"

"Yes Mrs. Yancey, it's me, " I said nervously.

"Thank you Lord, " she exclaimed. She was so glad to hear from me. *"I prayed that I'd get a chance to talk to you soon. How are you?"*

"I'm good under the circumstances." I didn't want her to keep feeling bad about what happened but at the same time, I had to be honest.

"How are John and Abby?" she asked.

"They are doing well also. John is playing basketball and Abby is bugging me about the prom already." At least I had that to be happy to report.

"Have you spoken to Grace about Mr. Yancey?"

"Yes ma'am. That's why I called. I'm so sorry." I couldn't find any other words.

"It's alright sweetie. By the time we found out, it had spread to other parts of his body. There was nothing anybody could do." I could tell Mrs. Yancey was crying.

"Mrs. Yancey, are you prepared for your husband's funeral?" I was too naive to do anything but ask more questions because I didn't know what else to say.

"Actually Irene, yes I am. Even though I could never get him to go to the doctor enough, he had no problems discussing his final wishes. I am fortunate that we talked about it many times. He already made arrangements to be cremated and when He's gone I'll be moving to Daytona Beach, Florida."

"Daytona Beach! Wow Mrs. Yancey, that sounds exciting!"

I could hear her chuckle. "Yes I suppose the beach is exciting for you young folks. I'm going back to my hometown to be closer to my family. I have two sisters and a brother there. Thomas asked me if I wanted to stay in Greensboro but I told him no and that I would like to go back south. So he bought a townhouse for me there already so my transition would be easy. I have to say he thought of everything. He made sure the house was paid in full and he's leaving me quite a large sum of money as well - about 3 million dollars. He's already sold the construction company and all the equipment. And he wants me to give away the two cars, the yacht, and the pick-up truck too."

Just then I heard what sounded like the doorbell ring.

"Irene I've got to go but there is so much more that I need to tell you. I can't tell you right away but will you please call me again," she pleaded.

My mind was already blown with what she'd already told me and she's telling me there was more? Before I could respond Mrs. Yancey asked again.

"Did you hear me Irene? Please promise me that you'll stay in touch. It is very important."

"Yes, of course Mrs. Yancey. I will."

"Thank you sweetheart. I've got to go now but we'll talk again soon."

"Yes ma'am."

"Bye bye now."

"Goodbye Mrs. Yancey." And then she was gone.

Grace was just walking into the door from her AA meeting.

"Grace!" I yelled. *"I'm in the living room."*

She looked me up and down as she rounded the corner into the living room. *"I can tell by the look on your face that you've spoken to Mrs. Yancey?"*

"Grace!" was all I could get out with my hands over my mouth. Of course she thought it was extremely funny. *"How much more do you know?"*

"Well, what did she tell you?" she asked curiously.

I quickly gave her the short version of what I knew and then I sat back in the chair Indian style waiting anxiously for her to tell me the rest.

"Well Rene, you know I wanted to tell you when she called me the day I texted you about Mr. Yancey but she made me promise to let her tell you herself so I did."

"I get it!" I said, waiting for her to continue.

"The doctors have given Mr. Yancey about a week to ten days to live. They have him on Fentanyl for his pain. Mr. Yancey's medical team wants to move him into hospice because there is nothing else they can do for him. He told Mrs. Yancey that he wanted to come home to die, so she is having an ambulance bring him home this coming Monday."

"Wow! That is a lot for Mrs. Yancey to handle. I hope she will be ok." I remarked sadly.

"We will see. They have been married almost forty years," Grace fired back.

"That's a long time. Mrs. Yancey didn't tell me he didn't have that much time left. I will call her again before we go to church tomorrow."

"Please do Irene. You know she is always constantly asking about you, John, and Abby. But there's something else."

"Ok," I replied curiously but I was thinking what more could there be?

"Mr. Yancey bought my parent's house, my house, the house next door to him. He made an offer to purchase directly from them when they listed it for sale for above their asking price and they accepted of course!"

I was astonished. No slight against Grace's house. It was a beautiful four bedroom home with a big backyard.

She continued. *"Mrs. Yancey said that Mr. Yancey left it to me and that it was all paid for!"*

"What! Oh my God Grace. That is amazing! I am so happy for you."

"Well that's not all. He's supposedly leaving me $200,000!"

"Oh my God Grace! You straight chick!" Grace was acting like she was not impressed.

"It sounds like a lot but I really deserve more when you really think about it."

I quickly agreed with her! I couldn't imagine all the terrible things that happened to Grace living next door to Mr. Yancey.

"Mr. Yancey is worth at least twenty million. He used to brag to me all the time that he could give me anything I wanted! I think he is doing this because he is dying and his guilt is kicking in now, that's all."

"Dang Grace. He is doing the most though for sure."

Grace sat down on the sofa. It seemed the conversation alone had become extremely draining for her so I just left it alone and we sat in silence for a few moments. Then she got up and ordered us two large pizzas and two foot long submarine sandwiches. I was really hungry too. I shook my head at Grace's vegan pizza. She even had Abby eating it. I just couldn't do it. I couldn't do that tofu stuff on my pizza.

It was Saturday evening by the time John returned from his game. I saved him some pizza because I figured he'd still be hungry. The snow had really started to come down again, pretty heavy and was sticking to the trees and the streets. John said that they won but it was a real close game. He also said that he fouled out with forty-three seconds to go! He said the other team's fans went crazy after he fouled out. He was devastated and their reaction just seemed to piss him off more.

"Calm down boy!" I told him as I hit him on the back of the head. *"Fouling out of a game is not the end of the world! And you all won. That's what matters. You are so blessed and fortunate to even be playing basketball. Be grateful."* Already Division One colleges and universities were trying to get John to sign with their schools. Malcolm taught me all about the division thang.

"That's easy for you to say sis. Never mind." And he sulked off to his room. You would have thought by his behavior that they lost the game. So I just left it alone and turned my attention elsewhere.

"Grace," I said, catching her off guard.

"Huh," was her reply as she was the one looking at me with curiosity.

"Would you consider going to church with us tomorrow? Actually," I interjected before she replied. *"I really want you to go with us!"*

It certainly was not an ultimatum. Grace was a grown woman, of course, but she could tell in my voice that I really wanted her to go. So could Abby because she even jumped into the conversation.

"Oh yes, please come with us Aunt Grace! Please, please, please!"

I wasn't sure if it was God, Abby's pleading, or if it was just the right time but Grace finally agreed to attend! This would be the first time in the two years we had been in Massachusetts that she would be attending church with us. I was so happy that I felt like I would break out in a holy dance!

Speaking of holy dancing, there were many Sundays during church service that I felt like doing a holy dance myself. I know Abby and John would be shocked if they saw that! I've shared this feeling with Malcolm a few times. Malcolm always tells me that by not doing what I feel, I am quenching the Holy Spirit. All I could respond was, "OK." I think fear more than anything was why I didn't follow through. I asked Malcolm whether he did the holy dance in prison? He said he did and so did a whole lot of other inmates. He explained to me that God's Holy Spirit and anointing was worldwide, even in the jungles of Africa and all third world countries! There was nowhere in the universe absent from His presence. Malcolm said that God used Pastor Nehemiah Washington, their prison Chaplain, to have the prison auditorium on Holy Ghost fire. Malcolm said that even some of the correction officers were praising the Lord!

I just hoped this Holy Spirit I felt at times would jump all over Grace! I didn't want it to scare her though where she wouldn't want to come back! Even though Grace wasn't scared of anything.

"Ok Grace! Then we can go pick out a Christmas tree after church?" I phrased it more as a question than a demand. I didn't want to push my luck in case she had something else to do afterwards.

"Yes, of course!" she replied happily. Abby let it be known that she wanted to go too! John with his nosey self, fresh out of the shower, yelled from his bedroom that he didn't want to go with us. It was so funny that Abby, Grace, and I broke out in a fit of laughter so hard at him!

"Chill out sir! I wasn't going to ask you to go anyway!" I yelled back. *"You are going to church with us in the morning though!"*

John was always trying to weasel his way out of going to church with us but I wasn't having it. The clean and sober mother of mine wouldn't have let John stay home either if she was alive. No, John staying home from Sunday worship was not an option. Even he liked to see the people at church do the Holy dance. He always came home and mocked how the folks were dancing. I always made him stop and go sit his silly butt down. Grace always got a kick out of watching John mock the people at church dancing and praising the lord. Now she might get to see it first hand.

With the afternoon winding down, I remembered I had some homework to catch up on. I'd changed two of my classes to on-line to free me up from having to go sit in a classroom after an eight hour work day and I mostly did those classes on my lunch break at work. The other two classes I had after work on Monday. I couldn't believe that I'd kept a 3.2 GPA with everything going on. I was basically operating like a single parent. I felt completely stretched out with work and John's home games during the week. But I had to keep pushing. It was my goal to become a Pediatrician. I wanted to treat children and Abby wanted to be a surgeon. I felt my Mother looking down on us from heaven. She would be so proud to have two daughters that were doctors. I didn't think John really wanted to do anything but be an NBA basketball player. He was always talking about how he was going to buy Malcolm and I a mansion wherever we wanted. I was thankful he was thinking of us but I always told him to just finish high school and the rest would take care of itself.

Of course, Abby was already doing her homework when I got to our room. I wasn't surprised. She was so studious.

"I haven't forgotten about your dress for prom," I told her. *"I'm just saving up a little more so you can get exactly what you want."*

Abby looked up from her books and said, *"that's great Irene! Since the prom is in late May, we can wait a little while."*

"That works for me!" In my head I was saying thank you Jesus because honestly I just didn't want to go out in the winter weather to look for anything. Because Amherst was a college town and there really weren't a lot of places to shop for women's dresses and formal attire. The women's clothing store downtown seemed to be for old bougie wealthy ladies. We certainly weren't going there. I would have to take her to the mall that was about thirty minutes from Amherst to a city called Holyoke. It was all highway driving to get there and I couldn't stand driving on highways! I remembered driving from Greensboro to Durham every weekend during my only semester at Duke. The drive was terrifying, but I did it. I couldn't take the back roads to Holyoke. The inner city was infested with drug addicts and driving through there was too dangerous. And we were not doing that! I was resigned to having to look there or even farther away in Springfield for something for Abby if we had to.

Abby finished her homework just as I was getting started on mine. Then she sat glued to the television screen binge watching the cheesy soap operas that aired during the week. It was the same cheesy soap our Mother used to watch when she was alive. That is where Abby got it from. Her boyfriend called twice but she told him she'd call him back both times. The second time I thought she was a little angry with him for disturbing her. I quietly laughed to myself but Abby looked at me at that exact moment as if she was saying without saying, *"Irene, what are you laughing at?"* I took the opportunity to tease her.

"Abby, why are you looking at me like that?" I asked. She didn't say a word but continued to watch her television garbage I called it.

Still teasing her I said, *"Oh, you're not going to respond?"* Abby looked up at me again and we both burst into a fit of laughter. We were true sisters with an unbreakable bond and I was grateful for that.

Since we were horsing around, I decided to bring John in on the action. I knocked on my bedroom wall. That was the signal for him to come to my room. He appeared after a few seconds.

"Is all of your homework done?" I asked.

John replied with an enthusiastic albeit sarcastic, *"Yeah Irene. I mean I did have a game today!"*

"John, don't play with me. If you start slacking with your school studies, you will be sitting out basketball for the rest of the season," I scolded.

"Quit worrying sis. I am doing everything I am supposed to do," he pleaded.

Then Abby punched him in the leg and asked, *"What are you doing right now boy?"*

"Abby quit playing," John said, *"I'm playing basketball on my Playstation."*

Then he stepped back and fired off at her again.

"Why are you questioning me Abby? You are not my boss!" he huffed, folded his arms, and settled into a lean against the wall.

"Both of you hush up now with all of that," I tried in a somewhat stern tone of voice. John responded with a mean frown and continued his pouting. Abby had a big smirk on her face.

"Can I go back to my room now?" John asked. I shooed him off with my hands. Abby and John liked to fuss from time to time. Heck, what siblings didn't.

"Abby, why are you always messing with your brother?" I asked.

"Because he always messing with me!" she fired back.

"You are fussing too much lately for my liking. You all are brother and sister. You've got to get along better than this. How many times

do I have to tell you that we are all we got? I need you to chill with all the fussing and picking."

Abby gave me a look like she was about to say something back. *"I'm not playing Abby!"* I said sternly.

Before she could respond her phone rang. It was Josh. I laughed because I remembered his name for a change. But the conversation didn't go like their usual conversations. Abby told him she was busy and to call her after church tomorrow. I could kind of tell by the look on her face and the tone in her voice that he wasn't too happy with Abby blowing him off.

He must have continued to nag her because at the moment she blurted out, *"I said I was tired, Joshua!"*

Then she said, *"Ok, ok! Be here at 9:30 in the morning and don't be looking like a hot mess!"*

When she hung up, I asked, *"Abby, is everything alright with you and Josh?"*

Abby replied, *"Irene, why did you ask me this?"*

"I can tell by the expression on your face," I replied gingerly.

"Josh is just being a bugaboo!" she huffed.

After I stopped laughing I asked, *"Why do you say this?"*

"Josh always wants to be around me. He gives me no time to breathe sometimes. It's suffocating."

"Well Abby, you are beautiful. Can you blame him for wanting to be around you? You have that long flowing hair and the way you're shaped, you look much older than seventeen," I interjected. *"Are you having sex yet?"*

"Heck No! Illky!" Abby quickly responded. *"Why would you ask me something like that!"*

"Because I was seventeen and I know how boys are. A lot of young boys just want to get into beautiful girls pants if they can! So are you sure you're not having those kinds of feelings for Josh?"

*"Well not me! I like Josh and all but I don't want to have sex...
at least not yet."*

I was relieved to hear it.

*"Good! There is no need to be in a rush. Besides your family, your
education is the most important thing in your life right now."*

Our Mother shared these same words with me. She knew
back then that Malcolm and I were very fond of each other.

"When was the first time that you and Malcolm had sex?" I was
shocked she asked. I started to tell her that it was none of her
business but I thought she was genuinely concerned about the
topic so I told her the truth.

"Abby, I was a virgin on our wedding night."

I don't know why I thought that would be the end of her life
of questioning.

She paused, *"how was it?"*

"Abby!" I couldn't believe her. I realized it was only because
I was slightly embarrassed to talk to her about me and Malcolm
specifically, but then I thought if she was going to find out about
sex, I would and should be the one to tell her.

*"Our Mother always told me to wait for sex until my wedding
night and that's what I did. She said that my husband would love
and respect me the most. But we will talk more about all this another
time."*

It was getting late. I asked Abby to turn down the television
so I could get to sleep and for her not to be watching too late as
well so she wouldn't be dragging in the morning getting ready for
service. I could hear that John's television was still on as well. I
knocked on the wall again.

He quickly emerged from his room and asked, rather annoyed,
"What is it Irene?"

I looked at him like he was crazy!

"You must think you're talking to Abby in that tone!" I fired back.

"I'm sorry," he quickly apologized because he could tell that I was heated!

"Turn your TV down and be in bed by midnight. You ARE going to church in the morning."

To that he responded, *"Why I cain't stay home with Grace in the morning?"*

"Boy, did you not hear our conversation earlier? Grace is going to church with us tomorrow!"

John's eyes grew wide as quarters, *"For real?"*

"Yes John, for real! Now go take out what you're wearing to church so you'll be ready on time."

Knowing there was nothing more for him to argue he simply responded, *"yes ma'am"* and went back to his room.

I could hear that he lowered the volume on his television and I settled in to get to sleep. Overall, I was grateful that both of my siblings were great kids. I was glad that John stayed away from the gangs at school. Trust me, the gangs were there but Malcolm stayed on John about staying away from them. John loved basketball too much and the possibilities it presented for his future so he was focused on going to college after high school and he seemed extremely dedicated to keep it like that! I was grateful because it was one less thing for me to worry about.

I laughed at John's bulging eyes when I reminded him that Grace was going to church with us in the morning. I grabbed my phone and texted her - we will be leaving promptly at 10:30 a.m. for church.

I saw the three dots. She was still awake.

I got an - **OK** 😊.

Abby was fast asleep in that short time. When I say she didn't mess around with her sleep, that was an understatement. The only time she had trouble sleeping was after we first moved here to Massachusetts. I knew right away it was because of what Mr. Yancey tried to do to her. The counseling helped Abby a lot. As my mind went back to that time, the feeling of hate and disgust I had for Mr. Yancey surfaced all over again. It didn't last too long though, especially knowing that he was expiring any day now. I prayed not to focus on the fact that part of me felt like he was getting what he deserved but to take it as a further opportunity for me to practice forgiveness. I always said *"I will forgive but I won't forget."* Malcolm got on me for saying this. I was thinking of that no good father of mine, Mr. Nathan, when I made that statement. Malcolm would say, *"Irene, you have to forgive your sperm donor as well!"* To be honest I still wasn't there yet.

After he was locked up I asked Malcolm if he had forgiven Mr. Yancey? He said yes and then he asked me what sitting around in prison festering on what had happened was going to do for him. He then told me holding grudges wasn't going to change anything. That was why I was so in love with Malcolm. At that moment I realized that I had to let Malcolm know that Mr. Yancey was dying. I wondered what he would say after I told him? I knew by Grace's reaction to my phone call with Mrs. Yancey that she didn't care that Mr. Yancey was dying. I really could not blame her. I did blame him though. I really believed she turned to a life of a lesbianism because of all the horrific rape trauma and molestation he caused. Then my mind wandered back to Mrs. Yancey. I remembered her plea for me to call her again. As I rolled over one last time, I thought I may give her a call tomorrow.

Chapter Twelve

The alarm woke me promptly at 7 a.m. This was my usual Sunday wake up time. After I got out of the shower, I headed downstairs. To my surprise Grace was already awake as well with biscuits, eggs, turkey bacon, apple sauce and hot chocolate made for our breakfast.

"Dang Grace! You made us a breakfast feast," I said jokingly.

I could tell she was nervous this morning.

"Well I figured we'd get something in our stomachs before we're sitting in church listening to the choirs of our bellies singing louder than the choir!"

She thought her joke was extremely funny and tried to give me a high five but I wasn't paying attention at that exact moment.

"Really," she, then, sounded annoyed.

"What happened?"

"You left me hanging," she said as she put her hand in the air again to show that I'd missed her high five.

"My bad," I tried to sound concerned but this was a little extra for Grace. But seriously, thanks for breakfast."

"No problem," she replied as we sat down to eat.

"Grace I didn't want to pry but how are things with your girlfriend?"

"As good as it's going to be I guess. We're good one day and back at each other the next. It's kinda up and down."

"Well it sounds like you all are at least cordial with each other and trying to work it out. Speaking of working it out, I promised Mrs. Yancey that I'd call her back."

Grace laughed and said, *"Yeah, you know she's always up and she's probably getting ready for church too,"* she said. Grace's eyes trailed off as if she were in a trance.

Mrs. Yancey went to church every Sunday morning when we lived with her. She was a member of the same church that Grace's parents were a member of when they lived there. Now that they were in Alabama, Grace called her parents every Sunday morning to check on them and see how they were doing. Her parents were retired with nothing but time on their hands now. Grace said that she knew she would have to answer a whole lot of questions from her mother concerning Mr. Yancey. Mrs. Yancey had already told Grace's parents that Mr. Yancey was dying! Mr. Yancey had already bought Grace's parents house. They both thought the world of Mr. Yancey. If they only knew the truth!

Grace got up from the table to make her Sunday morning call to her parents. I finished up my breakfast and trotted back upstairs to wake up Abby and John so they could eat, shower, and get dressed for service. We always left for church between 9:30 a.m. and 9:45 a.m. so we could get a good seat.

"Good morning Abby," I belted as I opened the window shades and let the sunshine in.

"Morning," she replied slowly as she turned over and pushed the comforter off.

"Grace made breakfast so get on up and wake up John so you can eat and shower."

She was happy for that news and quickly hopped out of bed humming *"I don't mind if I do!"*

I noticed that Abby started to take longer in the shower now that she was getting older. Grace was also teaching her how to apply make-up these days. I didn't think she needed make-up. She looked beautiful with or without it. I thought she was a natural beauty.

While everyone was scurrying around doing one thing or another, I escaped into the living room to call Mrs. Yancey. I knew she would be leaving in about an hour for her Sunday morning service. Mrs. Yancy also served as an usher two Sundays out of the month. I didn't know if this was one of those Sundays or not. Before he became ill Mr. Yancey usually took Mrs. Yancey to church. I wondered how different she felt having to be there without him. I dialed her number and she answered right away. Somehow she always seemed to answer on the first ring.

"Hello darling. How are you?" Mrs. Yancey answered in a happy voice.

"I'm doing fine Mrs. Yancey."

"How are the beautiful little Miss Abby and my little boyfriend John?" she sang.

I forgot she was crazy about John. Those two did a lot together when we lived in the Yancey's house. She bought him everything he wanted. At one time I felt like Mrs. Yancey thought John was her real son! John was really crazy about her too. She took him everywhere using the same Uber driver when we lived with her.

"Everyone is well! How are you holding up?" I asked.

"I'm actually doing great. I've lived a wonderful life with Thomas. We've been together forty years with thirty-eight of those years married and despite his shortcomings, he treated me like a Queen everyday. I was a virgin when we married and he is the only man I've ever been with. So I'm not sad."

She grossed me out with the virgin information but I knew it meant a lot for her to share with me so I kept listening.

I remembered Mrs. Yancey explaining to me when we came to live with her that she didn't have any children of her own because she miscarried twice. The doctors told her that she couldn't carry a child full term and performed a hysterectomy on her so she wouldn't keep conceiving. Mrs. Yancey said the doctors back then didn't know then what they know now. After she shared that with me, I had such a deeper love and respect for her. It made us having to leave her so much harder. She felt she was getting a second chance at children getting to take care of us. I felt so sorry for her. She really did take excellent care of us when we were with her. But as it stood, I guess it was all water under the bridge now.

"Abby is doing fine. She is the class president and will be graduating at the top of her class. John is getting tall. He is actually taller than me now. With him playing basketball and all, he is starting to look like a young man."

I knew Mrs. Yancey knew all of this information because Grace told me she told her these things but I was trying to make conversation knowing Mr. Yancey was quickly expiring. It brought back memories of when my Mother was quickly dying.

"You know Irene, I thought I was doing something sending you money. Thomas told me last week that he knew I was sending you $300.00 a month. He said there was no point in addressing it because he knew it was something I needed to do. He's actually shared a lot with me these last few weeks. He told me he checked on Malcolm from time to time. He found out that Malcolm built up a large prison ministry and the inmates really respected him."

I was trying to stay engaged with everything she was telling me but I couldn't help but wonder why he cared how Malcolm was doing since he put him there.

All I could muster up was a *"un huh."*

I knew Malcolm was locked up because Mr. Yancey was one of the most powerful black men in Greensboro and the State of North Carolina. He could find out pretty much anything he wanted.

Mrs. Yancey continued. *"You know Thomas gave me $500.00 to send to Malcolm. He told me not to put where the money came from and I did."*

"What! That was Mr. Yancey and you?"

Mrs. Yancey replied, *"yes it was."*

Before I could reply she added, *"and there is something more but I've got to go finish getting ready for church. The church van will be here to pick me up soon. I've got to see Thomas tomorrow but are you free Tuesday? We can continue then."*

"Sure Mrs. Yancey. "

"Ok. I'll talk to you later. Tuesday! Call me Tuesday!" Mrs. Yancey yelled.

Trust me, at that point I was blown away with what she'd shared and I didn't want to hang up. I wished I could call Malcolm immediately but I knew I couldn't. He wouldn't be calling me until Tuesday evening but it was a lot to process. So I decided to call my sister-n-law Jada.

I hadn't spoken to her in a while. I knew that Malcolm and Jada spoke every Sunday night though for a few minutes. I hadn't had the chance to tell Malcolm that Mr. Yancey was dying yet either.

Jada's job had relocated her to Minneapolis, Minnesota. That was quite far from us in Amherst, Massachusetts. She was torn about leaving us but I told her we'd be fine. She always texted and called to find out how we were doing. I always got back to her quickly so she would know we had everything under control. And we did! Jada had done enough for us so I made it my business not to bother her for anything! Plus, Grace was living with us which made things so much easier.

I hit Jada's contact in my phone. She answered almost immediately.

"Hello Sis," She sounded happy to hear from me.

"Hello there," I answered.

"How are you?"

"I'm good. Up and getting ready to go to church."

Jada asked quickly, *"Is everything alright? You don't usually call me on a Sunday morning."*

"Yes, everything is fine. I found out some news that I hadn't been able to tell you or Malcolm yet. I know you talk to him on Sunday nights and I wanted him to know before I get to talk to him on Tuesday."

"Sure Sis. What's up?" She sounded concerned.

"Mrs. Yancey called me. She's actually called a couple of times and each time she calls, she tells me something else I didn't know."

"Really?"

"Yes, she called me first to tell me Mr. Yancey is dying. The doctors have given him 7 to 10 days to live."

Jada was quiet at first and then she said, *"I am so sorry for her. How is she holding up?"*

"She's doing good. I just thought Malcolm would want to know sooner rather than later and I was hoping you'd let him know tonight."

"Absolutely, I will certainly tell him."

"Jada, did Malcolm tell you about the $500.00 someone put on his books?"

"Yes he did. We thought it was the Pastor who comes every weekend to minister to the inmates from an outside church - Pastor Nehemiah - because no name was attached to it."

"No it wasn't Pastor Nehemiah. It was Mr. Yancey."

"No way! For real?" Jada shrieked.

"Yep! For real! Mr. Yancey had Mrs. Yancey send it to Malcolm anonymously."

"That money was guilt money." Jada scoffed. *"Malcolm would definitely want to know this sooner rather than later. I know he'll be happy that at least he didn't keep it all for himself. He spread it out among the other inmates, especially those who didn't have any money at all. I'm going to put you on 3-way with me and Malcolm tonight Irene. I think he needs to hear all of this from you."*

I knew Malcolm called Jada every Sunday night at exactly 7:40 p.m.

"Ok Sis. Thank you. I'll talk to you tonight."

"Later Sis."

I hung up with Jada and quickly finished getting dressed so we could all head to church. We arrived and got great seats. One of the deacons came forward to do the morning prayer and the service started on time with the Praise and Worship team on fire as usual. The anointing was all over the sanctuary. People were crying and praising the Lord. I could see that this moment had also really moved Abby because tears were streaming down her face. Grace put her arms around Abby. I was so thankful I wanted to scream and let loose just one good time but I didn't. I guess I was quenching the spirit just like Malcolm told me I was doing but I couldn't figure out how not to do it. I could definitely feel God's presence very strongly, I just needed to know what to do with it!

As the spirit began to settle down, the praise dancers came out. They were always good. I could tell by her body language that Grace was having a good time. I was relieved. But my mind began to race with thoughts of my Mother, my father, the

Yancey's, school, Malcolm, Abby, and John. We had all been through so much and it felt like Mr. Yancey's death was opening up the wounds we had been trying to close and live with.

The choir took the stand and the music brought my thoughts back. I loved the choir. I'd actually thought about joining the choir on several occasions. But I was told I would have to audition in front of the choir director. That way he would know what section of the choir to place me in. I, myself, didn't know if I was an alto, soprano or tenor. The thought of auditioning has kept me from moving forward. Abby always teased me and said I sang in the basement, a new section. It was always a good laugh.

After the Pastor preached his sermon, he made an altar call. I asked Grace if she wanted to go up with me. Surprisingly enough, she did! The Pastor anointed everyone that came up for prayer with some olive oil he brought back from Jerusalem. I don't know what Grace went up for, but I prayed it worked. She was so adamant in the past that she didn't believe in God. I really think all that came from her dealing with the rape, sodomy, and disrespect from Mr. Yancey. I really believe Grace had come to the conclusion that if there was a God, He had certainly forgotten her. Oh, how I wanted her to know that was not the truth. I knew this for a fact because I believed God had not forgotten me, her, my siblings, or Malcolm. We left the altar and came back to our seats with tears in our eyes. I felt like after all the hell that we'd been through, I had to believe God was in control. I got a lot of my faith from Malcolm. His faith was crazy big. I knew I had to start believing off of my own faith now. I was hoping it would become as crazy big as Malcolm's.

Our ride home was lively. Abby asked Grace how she enjoyed the service. She said she was very surprised that it was so good. I was just glad that she enjoyed herself. John asked if she was going to come back. She said she absolutely would and that made everybody happy.

We all filed into the house and everyone pitched in to help make dinner. It was almost as if because going to church went so well, everyone wanted the togetherness to continue. As we sat down at the kitchen table for dinner, I said the blessing. Abby and John continued to talk about how great the service was from the praise and worship to the message. I wanted to ask Grace how she felt about the altar call but I didn't want her to be embarrassed so I figured I'd wait to ask her that when it was just the two of us. She did mention that she grew up in a church that preached heavily against Gays and Lesbians. She didn't know it could be any other way. She said she felt the love of God in the service and that made me scream, *"Hallelujah!"*

The church Grace was referring to was Mrs. Yancey's current church and the church Grace and her parents attended before her parents moved away. I told Grace that I knew there was a Gay couple in our church. Grace said she noticed that we had a few Gay people in our church. I thought to myself that Grace could probably pick that community out. I told Grace that God loved everyone and I wanted to leave it at that. I was not about to go into this topic like Malcolm would! Malcolm knew the bible scriptures that spoke against homosexuality. But I knew there were bible scriptures on just about every sin. I really didn't think God focused only on the sin of homosexuality. I mean there were thieves on the cross. There are people who don't pay their tithes and offerings which Malcolm also said was a sin and the list goes on and on. I just knew there were a lot of sins - the adulterer and the fornicator were all sins. All these folks did not get a free pass. I was just glad that Grace didn't have anything bad to say about my church this morning.

We all finished up dinner and the dishes together as well. I think we were so excited about the day that we all tired ourselves out. We all sat in the living room together and fell asleep watching television. Of course it was John who woke everyone up rummaging for food again in the kitchen. I didn't need to sleep too much longer anyway. I wanted to make sure I was ready when Jada called me with Malcolm.

Before I knew it, it was 7:35 p.m. and I was ready and waiting for Jada's call. The phone actually rang promptly around 7:42 p.m.

"Hello Jada!"

"Hello Sis. Malcolm is on the phone already."

"Hey baby!" I screamed.

"Hey my beautiful wife!" Malcolm yelled back.

"I know we can't talk long but I had to tell you that Mrs. Yancey has been calling me. She told me Mr. Yancey was dying and that he has about a week and a half or less to live."

"You kidding, right?" Malcolm seemed confused.

"No baby, You know I wouldn't kid about something like this," I chimed in.

"I feel so bad for him and Mrs. Yancey. When we finish our call, I'm going into the chapel to pray for him."

It blew my mind that Malcolm was going to pray for the man that had him locked up because of a lie. My husband had been imprisoned for nearly 3 years and he wanted to pray for the man that put him there because he was dying! At this point I started to feel like Grace. Bitterness was trying to creep into my body. I felt like I was becoming numb for a moment. I had to put myself in check because I was seriously almost ill with the fact that Malcolm wanted to pray for Mr. Yancey for real. I just wanted my husband home.

"I will be talking to Mrs. Yancey again on Tuesday but I wanted you to know this as soon as possible."

"I'm glad you did Irene. Thank you."

I quickly remembered that this was Malcolm and Jada's night to talk and not ours.

"I love you Malcolm. I'm going to give you back to Jada now."

"Jada, thanks for letting me use some of your talk time."

"No problem Sis. The Bureau of Prisons has a new phone policy for the Christmas season. Now all inmates have fifteen minutes of talk time instead of the usual ten minutes."

"Wow! Thanks Jada! We'll talk soon."

I hung up and my thoughts switched to the fact that I'd almost forgotten that Christmas was in thirteen days. I had to finish shopping for Malcolm. I had already bought him some Nike sneakers that he probably wouldn't wear in prison. But I wanted him to have something nice. I needed to get him some socks and boxers. Malcolm always teased me about buying him some tighty-whitey briefs. He told me not to buy them under any circumstances. Malcolm was adamant about this.

I didn't have any shopping to do for Abby and John because they only wanted money. They loved to have their own money plus, I knew they didn't want to hurt my feelings by saying they didn't want me shopping for them. Even though I am not that much older than them, they both say that I am a little old fashioned. I didn't argue with them because I knew there could be some truth in their statements. I had it honestly though. It came from our Mother.

My mother was old fashioned in a lot of aspects. Her moving here from Haiti in her teens probably had a lot to do with it. My Mother told me that when she came to America, people always teased her about the way she dressed and how she kept her hair.

She said that's why my father, Mr. Nathan, always took her shopping for clothes. He picked out things for her and showed her how to mix and match things together. Then he took her to the beauty parlor to get her hair done. My Father did all these things for my Mother. I reasoned that he must have loved her to do these things. I tried to include aspects of our Haitian Heritage in our lives so that Abby and John wouldn't forget. I always planned to visit Haiti one day to try to find any of our extended family members. I was sure we had some there.

Chapter Thirteen

Monday was a blur. So much happened over the weekend until my brain needed a day to not have to think about anything. I moved through the day seemingly at a snail's pace and attempted to bring some sense of normalcy to my thoughts. But it didn't work. At 3 a.m. Tuesday morning I was wide awake staring into my darkened room. I wondered what else Mrs. Yancey had to tell me. With everything going on knowing Christmas was eleven days away didn't feel so festive. It turned out my anxiety had me awake on purpose. Just then my phone lit up. I always put my phone on silent when I was sleeping yet now it was blinking which let me know it was a notification. Who was texting me at this hour? I picked my phone up and turned it over. As soon as it opened from my facial recognition Grace's text popped up across the screen:

YANCEY HAD MRS. YVETTE BRING HIM HOME YESTRDY. SHE WNTS US 2 FACETIME CAUSE YANCEY ASKED HER TO. SHE SAID HE DIDN'T HVE MUCH TIME LFT. #HELP

Was he serious? I couldn't believe it. Hadn't he taken Grace through enough? I can't do it. I'll just get up and go tell Grace that I can't do it. I slowly slid out of bed being careful not to wake Abby. I could see the light on under Grace's door. I knocked softly but I didn't hear any movement.

"Grace," I whispered while turning the doorknob and letting myself in the room. She was staring intensely at her phone with tears streaming down her face. Oh no! She'd already gotten on the call. I reluctantly sat down on the bed next to Grace, careful not to appear in the camera and put my hand on her shoulder. I could hear what sounded like Mr. Yancey was struggling to breathe. There he was lying in his bed with Mrs. Yancey sitting in a chair next to the bed. He had a nurse there with him. She was changing out his bag with the liquid hanging beside him. I was trying not to look but I couldn't help it. The man who caused us so much pain now seemed so fragile lying in that bed.

"Why won't you let the nurse add more pain reliever Thomas? You'll be more comfortable," she said as she patted his hand that was wrapped in hers.

He seemed to be refusing the medicine but he started struggling to talk. He was apologizing to Grace.

"Everything I did to you was wrong and I am so sorry!"

Grace just sat there and cried. Her sobs were audible now and she put one hand over her mouth.

Mrs. Yancey asked, *"Is Irene there Grace?"*

She simply nodded and turned the camera more toward me so that she could see that I was right next to her. Before I realized it, I had seriously mean-mugged Grace. I didn't want to see or talk to the Yancey's at this point!

"Talk to them!" Grace managed to speak in between sobs but with a slightly authoritative tone in her voice. I'd never heard her speak like that before. I grabbed the phone from Grace.

126

Mrs. Yancy said, *"Hello Irene."*

"Hello Mrs. Yancey."

Mr. Yancey moved around in the bed and starts trying to lean forward. Before the nurse could get over to him he started talking.

"Young lady, I'm sorry. I apologize for all the grief I caused to your family!" Mr. Yancey then pointed to some papers that were on the table beside the bed. *"Malcolm wrote to me on a few occasions. He said he has forgiven me for having him incarcerated."*

Then the tears started to stream down my face. I tried to look away but then Mr. Yancey broke out with a huge smile.

"He is an amazing young man!" He couldn't get anything else out after that. He started coughing so bad I thought he was going to choke to death right then and there. Mrs. Yancy took a towel and wiped his forehead and mouth. Mr. Yancey tried to say some more but he couldn't.

The nurse looked at Mrs. Yancey and said, *"You should do your final preparations. It won't be long now."*

Mrs. Yancey reached up and grabbed the phone from whatever was holding it up.

"Thank you girls for allowing him to do this. It was something he wanted very much to do. I'm going to let you go now. Good night."

She didn't wait for us to respond. She just hung up. I didn't know what happened while he was talking but I couldn't hold on to my anger anymore. Something inside of me felt like yelling, *"I love you Mr. Yancey!"* But I dared not knowing that Grace was still in pain over this man. Well we all were but hers ran so much deeper than ours. I was not about to tell Grace what I was feeling but at that moment I was feeling I didn't want this man to die.

Mrs. Yancey was being so strong. I couldn't believe how calm she was. I remember when my Mother died. I was a total mess!

I looked over at Grace as I wiped my face with my hand but the tears were still streaming from her eyes.

"Grace are you going to be ok?"

"Yes," she sobbed. *"But I don't want to feel how I'm feeling."*

"How are you feeling?"

"This man did all these hateful things to me for so many years and for years I've been cool with hating him for it. Now that he is dying, I couldn't take looking at him in his condition."

"I believe I feel the same way Grace. At this point, I don't want Mr. Yancey to die either."

I grabbed her and we held on to each other it seemed for dear life. We cried until we just couldn't cry anymore. And then we just sat in silence for a while.

All I could think about was how much more my amazing husband made me love and adore him. Malcolm never told me that he had written Mr. Yancey. I'm sure he thought I wouldn't understand and he would have been right. As much as he tried to teach me about forgiveness, it wasn't until this morning that I actually felt it. The whole situation was just mind blowing.

I realized it was almost 6 a.m. I had to get myself together. I knew I had to tell Abby and John that Mr. Yancey was dying. I doubted that they would really care but I was going to tell them anyway. This was their last day of school before Christmas break.

Abby was just waking up to get ready for school. I knocked on the wall for John to join us. He stumbled in all sleepy-eyed. Abby began laughing at him.

"Wake up John. I have something to tell both of you."

Abby stopped laughing.

"What happened?" John asked.

"I don't know how to say it so I'm just going to put it out here. Mr. Yancey is dying."

Abby's face seemed to turn a shade paler. John was confused. *"Wow. How?"* he asked.

"He has cancer and he is very sick. They don't expect him to live more than a few more days actually."

Abby still didn't say a word.

"Ok. Is that all Irene?"

"Yes, John. That is all."

John turned and left the room more orderly than he'd entered it. I looked over again at Abby and her expression was so stoic. I knew she was processing what I'd just told her so I left her alone. Mr. Yancey had this house in an uproar again. I wished he wouldn't have waited until his dying days to apologize to Grace. I knew he must have apologized to Mrs. Yancey for all the terrible stuff he had done that ultimately affected her. But Mr. Yancey did not apologize directly to Abby. I realized that that might not happen and that it was probably for the best. Anyway, I didn't want Abby to have a setback seeing him. She was doing amazing in school. This was her last year of high school and I refused to let anything derail my baby sister moving forward.

It was late and I was definitely tired. I turned off my brain and prayed that sleep would come quickly.

My prayers were answered. It seemed like as soon as my head hit the pillow I was out but 7 a.m. came faster than I would have liked. I got up, got ready for work, took Abby and John to school and did my regular Monday thing. Sunday's call with Mr. Yancey was still heavy on my mind. I was still tired and I don't know how I stayed awake in my Monday night class. Thank goodness the Red Bull I bought actually worked. After class I headed straight home and crashed. I knew I still had to talk to Mrs. Yancey on Tuesday unless something came up. With the Yancey's taking over all of our conversation on Sunday, I didn't get to tell Malcolm that Grace went to church with us on Sunday.

Tuesday began with more of the same. At least I got some great sleep so I felt rested. The professor for my Tuesday class was very strict and I was too scared of him to fall asleep. It was just an hour class so Grace usually had dinner ready when I got home from class. When I stepped through the door I could smell the night's menu. Grace made ribs, collard greens, and candied yams. John was already at the table eating.

"*Lord, we about to throw down,*" I said looking at the spread of food.

"*Where's Abby,*" I asked.

"*She hadn't come down yet,*" John replied, not bothering to look up from his plate.

I called Abby down to eat and then I asked John, "*Did Grace eat already?*"

"*Yeah, she just ate the collard greens and the candied yams.*"

Abby and I had started fixing our plates.

"*Yes Grace doesn't eat meat but she makes it for us,*" John smiled and then got up to fix himself another plate.

"*John! How many plates have you already had?*" I questioned.

He looked annoyed. "*Just one!*"

"*Alright then, carry on.*"

John came back to the table and said, "*Irene, I would never eat all the food from you, but, Abby, I don't know!*"

"*Be quiet!*" Abby yelled at John.

"*I'm just kidding. I wouldn't eat it all from you either.*"

The three of us laughed. I was glad Abby was herself and that she didn't go back into a shell over the news of Mr. Yancey dying. I guess her therapy really did work.

As Abby and John washed the dishes, I ran upstairs to take my shower and change my clothes so that I could be ready for Malcolm's call. I was excited about the extra time he would be getting. Our calls always seemed to end so fast.

I went into the living room for some privacy which is where I usually had my calls with him. 8 o'clock came and went and no Malcolm. I started counting the minutes. 8:05. 8:10. At 8:15 I started pacing. 8:20. 8:25. 8:30. I wondered what in the world had happened. I paced back to the bedroom clearly in my feelings. I could hear Abby in there talking to Josh. It seemed that he was fussing that he didn't get to come over tonight. Abby was letting him know that just because they were out of school for school Christmas break, he was not coming over every night and especially tonight. She told him Tuesday was the night I got to talk to Malcolm.

Just then John came out into the hallway.

"Irene, don't forget our regional championship game in Worthington, Massachusetts on Thursday."

"How far away is Worthington?"

"I don't know but I think it is far away."

"I'll find out."

"Suri, how far away is Worthington, Massachusetts?" I asked.

She answered back with her usual cheery self, *"Worthington is 48 miles from Amherst."*

"Ok that's not far at all John."

"That's good. The school is supplying two buses for family and friends since its the regionals and all. If you guys want to ride, I have to let the school know tomorrow."

"You know Abby and I will go but I'll have to ask Grace. That will save us from having to drive."

I sent Grace a text.

R U BZY? COME TO THE HALL.

She opened the door and said, *"Why are we meeting in the hallway?"*

131

"Abby is finishing her call with Josh and I was trying to give her some privacy."

"Awe, you are such a thoughtful big sister. What's up"

"John's last game is Thursday. You going?"

"Of course I'm going," Grace replied.

"We don't have to drive. They are getting a bus for family and friends."

"Well ain't that fancy!"

"I would say so," I said as we burst into a fit of laughter.

The laughter was short lived though as Grace's phone vibrated. She'd received a text message. Instantly her face went from a smile to a frown.

She looked up and said, *"It's Mrs. Yancey. Mr. Yancey just passed."*

We all just stood there speechless in the hallway. It seemed like we were standing there forever before Abby appeared in the doorway. Grace went back to her room.

"Why are you guys standing in the hall," she asked.

I didn't want her to think I was spying on her conversation with Josh so I avoided that route altogether.

"Mr. Yancey just passed."

I grabbed them, pulled them close to me and just held onto them.

"Are you guys ok," I asked.

"Yes," they both replied together.

"Are you," they asked me.

I knew they were sincerely concerned.

"I'm fine. Everything's going to be alright guys. We've survived this so far. And we will keep surviving it."

I went into the bathroom, turned on the shower, and just sat there. I didn't know what emotion I was feeling but it was a lot of them. I finally settled on worry. It was passed 9 p.m. and Malcolm had still not called. This had never happened before. I didn't know what else to do but pray. I prayed for Malcolm and I prayed for Mrs. Yancey. I prayed for Grace, Abby, and John and I prayed for myself. If I didn't know anything else at this point, I knew that God was a prayer answering God. Malcolm told me that even in the hard times I just had to keep asking, seeking, and believing.

I got up, turned off the shower, and went to bed. I decided I would text Jada in the morning and tell her Malcolm never called and see if she knew anything. At least now I knew why Mrs. Yancey never called.

We managed to get through Wednesday and Thursday without incident. I texted Jada Wednesday once I got to work, told her that Malcolm never called, and asked if she'd heard from him. Her reply was strange. She said she hadn't heard anything but that she would call the prison and inquire if he were in the infirmary or anything and let me know.

That was the last thing I needed. If anything had happened to Malcolm, I didn't know what I would do.

We showed up on time at the school to ride the bus with the other family members and friends of the players on the team. The bus ride was the worst of my life. I think I felt every bump! I knew I didn't have Hemorrhoids but that bus ride made me feel like I did. I just kept thinking that John had better win to make the ride all worth it. The game was a welcome distraction from the morbid thoughts of Mr. Yancey. Thankfully, John's team won the regional championship game. John really showed out with twenty-five points, seven rebounds and three blocked shots. Malcolm taught me how to keep all of his stats. He was the MVP of the game. He was all smiles as the reporters and cameras took pictures of him holding up the MVP trophy. I was so proud of him and I knew our Mother would be too.

Before I knew it, it was Friday. It was officially eight days before Christmas. Grace told me that Mrs. Yancey was cremating Mr. Yancey today and that they were having the memorial service at 6 p.m. in Greensboro. They were streaming it live on Facebook and YouTube. Grace and I decided to watch together. Abby and Josh went Christmas shopping at the mall in Holyoke. Josh's parents let him use their Mercedes SUV. He had proven to be a safe driver so I let him take them out from time to time.

There were a lot of people, including politicians and important wealthy businessmen at the service. The camera showed quite a bit of Mrs. Yancey. I wished they wouldn't have. She cried quite a bit. My heart went out for her and I wished I could have been there for her. She had been there for us after my Mother died. She was all we had and now I felt like I was abandoning her when it looked like she had no one else now either. I wasn't sure if because the service was scheduled at the last minute that her brothers and sisters couldn't be there for her. Mrs. Yancey really didn't have anyone there to console her. Some of her church members sat in the rows behind her but from what I could see none of the people chose to give Mrs. Yancey the consolation she needed.

Grace sobbed softly beside me. Her parents flew in from Alabama for the memorial and I could see them in the audience. They had been neighbors to the Yancey's for years. I wondered why they didn't console Mrs. Yancey? I didn't know if Grace had finally told them the horrible person Mr. Yancey actually was. At least I was glad Grace and I were able to be there for each other.

I was still tripping that I had not heard from Malcolm since our three-way call with Jada last Sunday. Malcolm usually called me like clockwork. I wondered what was going on. I thought about him all week. I thought about every aspect of our relationship from the time we met in that broken down apartment building we all stayed in up until now. I remembered when I actually knew I was in love with him. My Mother called it me being sweet on him and I tried to deflect but I was cheesing so hard that I did nothing but confirm her suspicions. Before long, though, she seemed to love him just as much as I did. I even became aroused thinking about our honeymoon. I really wanted Malcolm home especially with Christmas coming up. The reason for Malcolm's arrest, Mr. Yancey was deceased now but Malcolm probably wouldn't get out for another two years. It didn't seem fair.

Chapter Fourteen

It was 4 a.m. Saturday morning when my cell rang. Not a text message or a notification but several rings. I had the ringer on vibrate so it scared me awake. It was Jada.

"Hello Jada?" It sounded more like a question than a statement. I saw that it was her name across the screen but then again it was 4 o'clock in the morning.

"Irene, I need you to wake up and pack a couple of bags. You're flying to Greensboro for a couple of days."

"Greensboro? Is this about the Yancey's? Mrs. Yancey wasn't able to..." I didn't get to finish my statement before Jada cut in.

"I know you have questions but I can't answer them right now because we don't have a lot of time. I promise you when you get to Greensboro all of your questions will be answered."

"Ok," I said as I pushed the cover off, got out of bed, and slid into the bathroom all while trying not to wake Abby.

"Check your email. There is a confirmed ticket for you on Southwest Airlines that is scheduled to leave for Greensboro at 8:30 a.m. this morning which is why we don't have a lot of time. I'm going to cash app you some money. I need you to take an Uber to Windsor Locks, Connecticut to Bradley International Airport."

I knew where this was. It was thirty minutes over the Massachusetts border into Connecticut. I'd taken Jada there sometimes when she had to take work trips. But this was moving too fast for me! I had to take a deep breath.

"What about Abby and John?"

"I already spoke to Grace before I called you. She's agreed to look after Abby and John while you're gone. I'm sorry for doing things like this, Irene but what's happening is very important and there was simply no other way."

"I understand," I said, fully awake now.

"Ok then. I've got to go because my flight to Greensboro leaves in about an hour from Minneapolis. So I'll get there before you. I'll send you enough money to get an Uber to the hotel. I'll text the hotel information in a few. See you soon."

"See you," I said, my voice trailing off. Now I was really baffled. I felt like Jada was acting too strange. I just hoped there was nothing wrong with Malcom. Not getting to talk to him during our regular scheduled time had me in complete knots. I hoped he hadn't gotten into any trouble. He often told me how some of the correction officers could be a pain in the tail. He said they could have you sent to the hole. Although Malcolm never got sent there, he told me about the hole from what the other inmates told him. Their description was that it was always cold and dark. There were big rats down there too. The bed was a hard thin piece of board on the floor with one thin sheet. Just thinking about those conditions made me hope more that Malcolm hadn't gotten into any trouble. He always said that there were some guys there that didn't like him, but he stayed away from them as best he could.

After I got out of the shower and headed back into the bedroom to get dressed and packed, I saw that Abby was waking up. I turned the lamp on beside the bed so I could see her.

"What's going on Irene? What time is it?" she asked.

"It's about 4:45 in the morning," I said as Abby sat up in bed.

She looked around the room and saw that I'd grabbed my duffle bag and suitcase from out of the back of the closet.

"You going somewhere," she asked.

"Yes baby sis. I'm going to Greensboro."

"Greensboro? Is something wrong with Mrs. Yancey now?" she asked.

"No Abby. Jada just called me and told me to get dressed and head to the airport. She said she couldn't tell me anything else but just get to Greensboro and she would tell me the rest when I get there."

Abby, being the eternal optimist, said, *"You're probably finally going to get to go to the prison with Jada to see Malcolm for a short visit."*

"Wow Abby! With Mr. Yancey dying this week and his funeral and everything that never even crossed my mind."

Trust me, I wanted to call Jada right back to find out what was going on. I wanted to know the reason we were flying home. I wanted to know why I hadn't spoken to Malcolm this week. I had so many questions. I was just thankful that Abby seemed cool with me leaving for a while. I had only been away from her and John during the week during my first semester in college. We were at the Yancey's then and I thought Abby and John were in their safe care. I didn't know what I didn't know.

Just then there was a knock at the door and then the door opened before I could say, "Come in." I figured it was Grace.

"I guess you're telling Abby what's going on?" she asked.

"Actually I'm just telling her that I'm going to Greensboro because that's all I know. Jada said she called you too? Did she tell you anything else?"

"No, she told me she needed me to do her a huge favor and look after Abby and John because she needed you to fly to Greensboro this

morning. *She apologized for it being short notice but that things were happening so fast that she was trying to make sure she helped you have no objections about getting on that plane."*

"But I do have objections, Grace! First of all there is the 'I don't know what's going on' objection. Then there's the 'I don't like that I don't know what's going on' objection. And oh yeah, there's the 'I've never flown on a plane before' objection. Is that enough objections for you?"

Grace knew I wasn't mad, I was just frustrated because I didn't know anything and I hated being left in the dark.

"Irene didn't you tell us everything was going to be alright?" she asked. There was the wind being let out of my sails.

"Yes I did," I replied reluctantly.

"Well then we've all got to believe that it is going to be alright and that everything will become clear when you get there."

"Well, thank you Grace. That makes me feel much better," I said. I was amazed at the way she spoke with wisdom and confidence. I couldn't tell if it was her faith talking or if she actually knew something I didn't know. But nonetheless, I left it alone and finished packing and getting dressed.

Before I headed down the stairs I headed to John's room. I knocked on the door but I didn't hear anything. I could see a light flickering under the door. I turned the knob and proceeded into the room. John was sitting up in bed with his headphones on playing his video game.

"Irene, you scared me!" he said.

"Boy!" I said knocking his headphones off of his head.

He asked, *"Irene, what did I do?"*

"How many times do I have to tell you that you can't hear me calling you or anything else if you've got these headphones on? Get out of that bed."

John looked at me with fear in his eyes.

I laughed at him and said, *"Boy, you haven't done anything wrong. I just need to talk to you,"* I explained.

"Oh, ok," he said, relaxing.

"Something came up and I've got to fly to Greensboro. I'll probably be gone no more than a couple of days but I don't know for sure because Jada wasn't able to tell me everything over the phone. Grace will be in charge while I am gone and you are to do what you are supposed to do just as if I was home. I know you're on Christmas break but don't be hanging out with anybody that's going to get you into any trouble. Remember what Malcolm always told you. Once I get there and get more information I'll call you guys and let you know. Now can I trust you to do what you're expected to do?"

John said, *"Yes, of course Irene."* I gave him a big hug and kiss.

"You are my baby brother and I am so proud of you," I said. Then I looked around John's room. "John, clean this room today. It looks terrible. You've got clothes and sneakers everywhere. Spray some Lysol too dude! It smells like a locker room in here!" I turned and walked out of his room.

At 6:30 a.m. I was downstairs and ready for pickup to the airport. The Uber app showed my driver fifteen minutes away. Grace was waiting with me in the living room.

"Grace I hope you know how much I love and appreciate you. You are my sister from another mister for sure. I'm so grateful that you're here with us and for your willingness to look after my Abby and John. You know they are all I have in this world as far as blood related," I said.

"Well I feel the same way about you, Abby, John, and Malcolm. You all are really all I have as well. My parents are still alive but they don't really know me like you do. They know the person I try to be in front of them to make them happy but they have no idea who I really

am. You do and you love me anyway and I love you for life," she said as the tears began to flow.

Her words touched me and I started to cry. I yelled for Abby and John to say goodbye as the Uber pulled up. They both ran into the living room and into my arms more like they were my own children and not just my siblings. I hugged them both and said, *"take care of each other because we are all we have. I know Grace is in charge but you guys look after her too, ok?"* They just nodded yes and I hugged and kissed everyone again.

"Ok John, help me take my bags to the car."

I stepped out into that cold Massachusetts air. One thing was for sure, if you weren't awake before you walked out the door, the cold would make sure you woke up really fast. We had already had a couple of snows and it was cold enough that the snow didn't melt. It just became a hard brick on all the areas that weren't plowed. John hated these winters because he was the one who had to come shovel the snow off of the porch and the driveway.

On the ride to the airport my thoughts began to race. I was shaking like a leaf hanging on a tree in a windstorm! Questions popped up in my mind. "Girl, what are you doing? Why did you leave your siblings behind? What if Grace decides to start drinking again?" The more I tried to shake them off the more it seemed they came flooding in. I had to get myself together. Satan was trying to chump me off! I remembered what Malcolm taught me about spiritual warfare and I started pleading the blood of Jesus against him and coming against every negative thought. Before I knew it, we were arriving at the airport. Just as I'd gotten rid of one set of fears another set came creeping in. The fact was I had never flown on an airplane before. My conversation with Jada happened too fast for me to offer that up as a deterrent for my trip. Plus she led with the fact that everything was already paid for so it was a little too late for me to back out from getting on this flight now. I looked down at my cell as I was getting out of the Uber. Jada was texting asking if I'd gotten to the airport yet. I still had my cell on silent, so I didn't hear the text notification. I quickly texted her back letting her know that I had just arrived at the airport and was about to check in.

The Uber driver pulled up right in front of the Southwest Airlines terminal. As soon as I got out of the car this nice man in a uniform grabbed my suitcases that the driver had taken out of the trunk and sat on the curb for me.

"*What flight are you taking,*" he asked me.

I pulled up the text message Jada sent.

"*I'm on flight 1705 to Greensboro, North Carolina,*" I replied.

"*May I have your name,*" he asked.

I told her my name and showed her my driver's license.

"*I'm sorry I'm so nervous. This is my first time flying,*" I explained.

She said, "*no need to apologize, you are fine. We'll take good care of you.*"

The desk attendant was so nice. Her words made me feel a little at ease.

"*You'll be leaving from gate A7. Boarding will start in about thirty minutes,*" she said, handing me my tickets and my driver's license.

"*Thanks,*" I gratefully replied. I proceeded to the security checkpoint and then to the gate. My heart was beating so fast. It felt like it was going to jump out of my chest.

As I sat at the gate waiting for boarding, my phone rang. It was Abby.

"*Yes ma'am,*" I answered.

"*Irene, I'm just calling to check on you.*"

"I'm so glad you did. Is everything alright?"

"Yes, we are fine. I know this is your first time flying and you are scared. I just wanted to make sure you're ok," she sounded like she was laughing.

"Are you picking on me Abby? You have some nerve. You've never flown before either missy," I replied. *"Everything is fine so far. I'm getting ready to get on the plane but I'll call you as soon as I get there and find out what's going on."*

"No problem. I love you and I'm saying a prayer for you," she said.

"Thank you Abby. I love you too," I replied.

I jumped in the line to board when my zone was called. When I got to the door of the airplane I told the flight attendant that it was my first time and that I was a little nervous. She welcomed me and showed me to my seat next to the window. She said I'd be just fine and if I needed anything to push the orange button above me and someone would come see about me. I didn't know if I would want to look out of the window or not once this big boy took off. I tried to settle myself.

The plane filled up quickly and we took off. I was holding on to the seat so tightly I think I cut off the circulation. Man, that rush was something else! I was up in the air for the first time in my life. So far it was not that bad. I looked out the window and the landscape was amazing. I just knew I would have to do it again with John and Abby. Just then my thoughts wandered to my Mother. I believed she was watching over me from up in heaven. At times like these is when I missed my Mother the most.

I figured out how to connect to the wifi onboard the plane. At 10:30 a.m. Jada texted that she had landed and that she was already at the hotel. I was to take another Uber to the Four Seasons Sheraton Hotel and come to room #1804. Then she said we had a busy day ahead and she'd see me soon. I sent her a thumbs up emoji so she would know I got the message. About an hour later, the Pilot spoke over the Loud speaker that we were landing and the flight attendants walked through the aisle to make sure everyone had everything put away for landing. From out of the window everything that looked far away was becoming closer. I could make out houses and buildings and cars moving. Then the plane finally landed and I held on tightly to the seat again as the plane slowed all the way down. Man, oh Man, that rush from the landing was just as intense as the take off. As we pulled into the gate, my mind wandered to thoughts of my no-good father, Mr. Nathan. The landing reminded me of when he took us to Disney World in Orlando, Florida. It felt like a ride on one of the roller coasters.

I managed to get off the airplane and find my way to baggage claim to get my bag. The Greensboro airport was pretty crowded. I guess it was because of Christmas being in about a week. I grabbed my bag and headed to the shared ride pick up area. My wait for the Uber wasn't long at all. As we were on our way I remembered this hotel being near the Four Seasons Town Center Mall. I didn't know how busy we'd be but I hoped I'd get a chance to shop. I wanted to get Grace something nice for Christmas. Grace had been everything to my family. And of course, I couldn't forget about Jada. My sister-in-law was heaven sent. We couldn't have survived our first couple of months in Massachusetts without her. I wanted to get her something too. Thinking about gifts for Grace and Jada led me down a rabbit hole as I thought about two friends on my job I want to give something to.

I decided to send Grace a text to let her know I'd landed and that I was on my way to the hotel.

Grace: Ok, have a good time. Can't wait to hear all about it. Gotta go. Sitting here in the kitchen spanking Abby and John in Uno.

I got a chuckle out of that. I knew John was ill if he was losing. He thinks he is the best Uno player ever. Teenage boys!

The ride from the airport to the hotel was only about fifteen minutes. When I arrived, I was so excited to see Jada. It had been a while since we'd seen each other. As I walked into the hotel, I found my way to the elevators. I took the elevator to the 18th floor and went to Jada's room, #1804. I knocked on the door.

I heard Jada ask, *"Who is it?"*

I said, *"It's me Irene."*

Jada opened the door. I walked in, put my bags down, and we hugged each other. It seemed like it was awhile before we let each other go.

"It's so good to see you," she said.

"It's good to see you too sister!" I said back happily.

All of the sudden, the bathroom door opened and out walked Malcolm! I gasped! All the blood rushed to my head and I fainted! When I came to, Malcolm was picking me up, sitting me on the bed and Jada was handing me a bottle of water. They were both laughing at me, something fierce. I reached up and grabbed Malcolm and held on to him so tight.

"Oh my God, you look and smell so good!"

Malcolm said, *"My love. It's been a long time and you looking good too baby."*

Tears were running down my face. I just couldn't believe it. My husband was right here in front of me. I felt like I was dreaming but I did not want to wake up. Tears began to fall down his face as well. Jada started crying at our reunion. We three were a bucket of joyous tears. I finally knew this was what people meant when they said, *"what a Kodak moment!"*

Jada said, *"I'm sorry sister. Things happened so fast and we figured the fastest way to get you two together was for you to come here."*

"Oh you don't EVER have to apologize for this, not ever!" I said almost screaming. And we all fell into a fit of joyous laughter.

"Are you ok?" Malcolm asked. He was holding my head in his hands.

"Everything is alright now!" I joyously replied.

Malcolm said, *"Before I tell you everything, let's first say a prayer of thanks to God."*

"I think that would be fitting," I agreed.

He began, *"Father, we want to honor you this morning. We thank you because you are Elohim, the Most High God and there is no other like you Lord. Please forgive us of any sin we've committed knowingly and unknowingly. We want to thank you for life, health, and strength. We want to thank you for the full activity of our limbs. We thank you Lord for this joyous reunion. Lord, nobody in this world could do this but you. We will always remember to bless your Holy Name. We ask that you please send your security Angels to cover Abby, John, and Grace. Cover all of Jada's friends too, Lord. Please look on and protect Mrs. Yancey as she embarks on a new life without her husband. Lord look on and protect the inmates and correctional officers at Caledonia State Prison. And last but not least, God, have mercy on Mr. Yancey's soul. In Jesus Name, amen and amen!"*

I immediately hugged Malcolm again. All I could think at that moment was that he was a real man. The first thing he wanted to do was pray! I was constantly learning from him forever.

Just then Jada interjected, *"Ok you two lovebirds. As much as I love this family reunion, I'm going to step out for a few. I'm having lunch with some of my friends from high school. I rented a car so I should be back in about three or four hours. Irene Malcolm knows this but the room next door is actually mine so you can mess up both of the beds in here."*

I started laughing and said, *"How very thoughtful of you sister. We sure will!"*

As soon as Jada left the room I realized, it was just Malcolm and me. I said to myself, *"Oh my God."* I became nervous immediately and my body began to shake and quiver a little. I couldn't believe this was happening; that my husband was standing right in front of me.

Malcolm said, *"Honey, you are so gorgeous."*

I was looking at all of him.

"Malcolm, you are huge. Look how big your chest and arms are. You don't know how much I prayed for this moment and it is finally here."

"Trust me," he said. *"I don't know what to do with myself either baby."*

"Malcolm, how did all of this happen?" I asked Malcolm.

"Sit down right here beside me and I'll explain." He grabbed my hands and started his explanation.

"Over a year ago God put it on my heart to write Mr. Yancey a letter telling him that I forgive him. Even though Mr. Yancey lied about the whole situation, I truly needed to forgive him for my own sake. Of course, I didn't receive a response so I mailed another letter telling Mr. Yancey that I had forgiven him. It was during that same time that Pastor Nehemiah Washington came into the prison that same week, as he did from that time until present every Sunday morning at 8 a.m. and he preached a powerful message on forgiveness and how we needed to forgive and release those who mishandled and spitefully used us. At first it scared me that God would give me a sign about what I did was right. It was confirmation from God through Pastor Nehemiah's message. Then I started writing Mr. Yancey twice a month. My letters detailed everything about me. I wanted him to know exactly who I was. I let him know how hard it was for Jada

and me growing up in a single parent household. I told him that my father raised Jada and I until he died of complications from diabetes when I was twelve years old. I told him that we really never knew our mother because she ran the streets. I told Mr. Yancey that my sister Jada raised me after my father died. I shared with him that my father was a Deacon in the church and that he kept Jada and I in church two times a week and all day Sunday. I told Mr. Yancey that I was a good student with a full scholarship out of high school to play basketball, football and baseball in Greensboro. I told him that I could have gone to college anywhere in the country, but I chose to go to North Carolina A&T in Greensboro so I could stay near my sister, Jada. I told Mr. Yancey that I was being scouted by professional NFL teams. I told him that you and I grew in the same apartment complex from little kids and that you and I, baby, have been in love with each other before we even knew what love was. I told him that we were both virgins until our honeymoon night. Mr. Yancey already knew your family's history from his wife and your mother meeting while they volunteered and ministered to the homeless and less fortunate. I let Mr. Yancey know that even though I shouldn't be in prison, that I was making the most of my time ministering to the inmates inside Caledonia, and that God was using me mightily. I wanted him to know exactly everything he took from me; from us. I knew with him being the powerful businessman and politician he was here in Greensboro, he would be able to confirm everything I wrote to him about me.”

"*Oh my God Malcolm,*" was all I could reply to the first part of his story.

He continued, "*Irene, check this out. Mr. Yancey became ill with Stage 4 cancer back in March of this year. The doctors told him then that there was not too much they could do for him. The cancer had spread all over his body. I told Mr. Yancey that I was* *sincerely praying for him. Baby, I believe God began to deal with Mr. Yancey. No, let me change that. I know God dealt with him. Today is evidence! Some Corrections Officers who I was cool with started hinting to me that Mr. Yancey had begun to put things in motion to get my release. Mr. Yancey was the one who sent that $500.00 to put on my account. I split that money up between four of my closest friends inside. Anyway, Mr. Yancey was quickly expiring and he put heavy pressure on the right people to get my release quickly. Then he wrote to me and told me that I would be getting out soon and that he was forever sorry for what he put me through. He apologized for taking Mrs. Yancey away from you, Abby, and John and asked that we always stay connected to her and check on her because she loves you guys so much."*

Malcolm let my hands go, went to his suitcase and grabbed some papers that were inside.

Then he said, *"Now baby, I want you to look at this certified document he sent me."*

He handed me a set of papers. It was Mr. Yancey's final will and testament. In it, he left Abby and John each $200,000 for college. He left Malcolm their house in Greensboro, the summer home in Myrtle Beach, all his vehicles and $10 million dollars. I blinked a couple of times to be sure I read that figure correctly and instantly became lightheaded again and felt as though I was going to pass out. Malcolm saw my face turn almost white and knew I was about to pass out again. He fanned me with the papers and put some pillows behind me.

"It's going to be o.k. Irene. Here drink," and he handed me the bottled water I started drinking when I passed out the first time.

"Did you know about this before now?"

"No, it was given to me with the rest of my things when I got released this morning. Jada spoke with Mrs. Yancey and she told

her that they were in full agreement of everything listed here. Their attorney drew up the will and I spoke to Mrs. Yancey this morning as soon as I got out. She said in all of their calculations, they forgot to bless Jada with something. I asked her if it was alright if I gave her $1 million from the $10 million she gave us. She told me, "Son, it's your money now. If that's what you feel, you go right ahead." It was Mrs. Yancey who told Jada Mr. Yancey's diagnosis."

I could not believe what I read and what I was hearing.

"Malcolm, this is way too much for me to process."

"Slow down Irene and just breathe," Malcolm told me.

John and Abby! *"I need to call Abby and John to let them know I am sitting here with you!"*

Malcolm laughed and said, *"Go ahead."*

"Oh no, I need to FaceTime her. She will never believe me," I said as I picked up my cell from the bed and dialed Abby's number.

Abby answered, *"What's up my big Sis?"*

Then she saw me wipe my eyes and she got nervous and said, *"Irene what's the matter?"*

"Everything is fine Abby. You'll never guess who I'm with," I said with a growing smile on my face.

"Who," Abby asked.

I turned the camera so that she could see Malcolm in the frame.

"Malcolm," she screamed. Then she asked, *"you went to the prison to visit him?"*

"No Abby," I said. *"It's better than that. Malcolm is out!"*

Abby yelled, *"No way. Oh my God!"*

Abby took off running to John's room where he was playing Madden NFL.

"Abby, what is going on?" he asked, confused.

Abby said, *"John, guess what? Irene is with Malcolm right now."*

John's eyes became real wide.

He yelled, *"Word?"*

Abby said, *"Word!"*

John said, *"Irene put Malcolm on the speaker phone."* He hadn't looked up to see that Malcolm was on FaceTime.

"We're on FaceTime John," I said.

John, finally looking up, said, *"Hey Malcolm, you really free?"*

"Yes lil bruh, I'm out" Malcolm confirmed.

"Hi Malcolm," Abby yelled.

"Hey baby girl," Malcolm said excitedly.

They were all so happy.

"I can't wait to see you both soon," Malcolm told them.

"We can't wait to see you too in person! When will that be," Abby asked.

"We're still ironing out the details, baby girl but I promise it will be sooner than you think," Malcolm said.

John yelled, *"Yeah so I can beat you in Madden NFL."*

Malcolm said, *"Ok John. I see you!"*

"Alright guys, let's let Malcolm get some rest. We'll check in on you later. Abby tell Grace I'll call her later."

"Ok Irene. Later Malcolm," Abby said.

"Later baby girl" Malcolm said. He acted more like her father than a brother and they loved each other as much.

It seemed like time stopped. We just lay there holding each other watching reruns of the Maury Show. I forgot Malcolm loved that show.

After a couple of hours, Malcolm sat up and said, *"Wifey, let's take a shower together. I need to visualize my wife naked instead of the gross naked men I've had to shower with for almost three years."*

"Ok baby," I said as I jumped up. *"Absolutely anything you like."*

Chapter Fifteen

It seemed like time stood still as Malcolm and I reconnected. I pinched myself several times to make sure I wasn't dreaming. And when I wasn't pinching myself, I was praying that I wasn't dreaming. After a couple of hours in each other's arms, Malcolm and I fell into a deep sleep. We were awakened only when the phone rang a little after 6 p.m. It was Jada. She was back from her outing and wondered if we were hungry.

Malcolm said, *"Of course sis. I've worked up a voracious appetite. But we'll probably just order room service so come on over."* Malcolm hung up the phone and said, *"Baby get decent. Jada is on her way over."*

I jumped out of the bed and grabbed Malcolm's shirt. I was just getting it buttoned up when Jada knocked on the door. Malcolm pulled his pants on and opened the door. I really think he was trying to arouse me some more. I think Jada noticed it too.

Jada saunters in our room and instantly looks at me. I tried not to look at her.

She said, *"Girl, why you looking down at the floor?"*

"What," I replied.

We both started laughing.

"You look like you're on cloud nine, ten, eleven, and twelve!"

Malcolm grabbed me and swung me around.

"She should be on cloud whatever she wants to be on 'cause she's here with me," he said, putting me in a bear hug.

We sat down on the bed and Jada stood in front of us with her hands on her hips and said, *"I would say get a room but I'm in it!"*

We all broke out in another fit of laughter.

"Seriously though," she continued. *"I'm so glad that God saw fit to bring us all back together again. This day has been a long time coming but our prayers have finally been answered. God will never leave you or forsake you if you live right!"*

"Hallelujah and Amen to that!" I chimed in. I felt the tears coming so I had to pull myself together.

Malcolm said, *"Ok you two. No more with the mushies. Let's order something to eat."*

Malcolm ordered a steak with a baked potato. He said he had been wanting steak for three years. Jada ordered a burger with fries and I ordered pizza. I still sat at the little round table in that hotel room looking at my husband in total shock and disbelief that he was really sitting right beside me. But it was real. He was real and he was there.

While we were eating, Malcolm and Jada got me caught up to speed on everything that had transpired. Jada had spoken to Mrs. Yancey at length since Mr. Yancey's passing and they were able to organize Malcolm's release and everything. Jada knew about the will and everything Mr. Yancey left to everyone. She said that's why she was able to take the time off of her job because her brother had just made her a millionaire and she was praying about what that meant for her career and her future. We were all meeting Mrs. Yancey at the bank on Monday morning to make the transfers and have the deed transferred and the titles to the cars. Malcolm said he still didn't know how to feel about it all.

I told him, *"Malcolm, this man lied on you and stole years of your life, of our lives that we can't get back. Your scholarships for school and your football career, you can't get that back. You have a record..."* He put his finger over my mouth and stopped me mid sentence.

"Ssshhhh baby. No more worries. God will restore all of that to me. I'll be able to go straight pro now. None of that has changed. We're still in God's timing. Stop fretting. It's all working together for our good. We're going back to Massachusetts because I know you want John and Abby to finish out the rest of their school year there and then we'll transition back here and resume our lives just the way God intended," he said, as he put his hand on my shoulder.

I knew he was right and his words began to settle and calm my anxieties and fears. But my mind went straight to Grace. I hoped she would be just as happy as we were that Malcolm was home and not feel like a third wheel. I wasn't sure if she would even want to come back to Greensboro. I knew she wasn't going to keep her parent's house. It held too many bad memories. I just knew I didn't want to lose her.

Then Malcolm said, bringing me out of my fog of thoughts again, *"As a matter of fact, I would like to visit our church for service tomorrow. "*

Jada said, *"Well I had already planned on going and I knew you'd want to be there too!"*

Malcolm responded, *"We'll be dressed and ready by 10:30 a.m."*

"Sounds like a plan," she said as she stood up, grabbed up the last of her fries and headed out the door.

Malcolm said he was going outside for a few just to be outside.

I understood what that meant. He'd been locked up for three years and he just wanted to exercise his freedom to be anywhere he wanted to be. I decided to go take a shower and lay down for the night. I was exhausted from this awesome crazy day.

I texted Grace to see if she was awake. She called me instead of texting back.

"Girl, I been waiting for you to call me all day! Oh my God, is it true? Malcolm is out," she asked, talking a mile a minute.

"Yes Grace it's true," I replied.

"Well I knew it was true. John and Abby said it was true. And I knew there would be no other reason why you wouldn't have talked to me by now," she kept talking a mile a minute.

"Grace!" I raised my voice. She was finally silent. *"Calm down."*

She started laughing and I laughed too.

"I'm sorry Girl. It's just so exciting around here. We are so happy. John and Abby haven't argued all day! You should see them Irene, they have been like two peas in a pod," she said happily.

"Well I know that's God! I'm so grateful to you Grace for being there for them, for us."

"You're stuck with me now and I'm not going anywhere!" she said happily.

"That's good to hear," I replied.

I caught her up on everything that had happened all day and what the plan was so far for the rest of the week.

She said, *"Don't worry. The house will be spotless and ready for you and Malcolm's return."*

"Ok Grace. We're going to church tomorrow and we'll see Mrs. Yancey on Monday and we'll probably be back either Tuesday or Wednesday but I'll let you know for sure."

"Get back safe. I love you sister."

"We will. I love you too and thank you again," she replied.

We ended our call just as Malcolm was walking back into the room from his walk. He walked over to me and put his arms around me and held me tightly. I sighed. I was finally in his arms again.

Sunday morning came quicker than I expected. I slept better than I'd probably slept in three years. I looked up into the eyes of my handsome husband who seemed like he was already awake and was watching me sleep.

"Good morning gorgeous," he said as he moved the hair from my eyes.

"Good morning to you my handsome husband," I replied.

"How'd you sleep," he asked.

"I slept great. How about you," I said.

"I didn't remember that a real mattress felt this good," he replied.

"I'm so sorry baby," I said, sorrowful.

"No apologies necessary wifey. It's all good. Remember what I told you last night. I'm just getting my bearings back. My body will remember what everything feels like in just a little while," he explained.

"What time is it," I asked.

"A little after 7 a.m. Let's go downstairs and eat breakfast," he said.

"Breakfast sounds good. I'll text Jada," I said as I grabbed my phone and headed to the bathroom.

We met downstairs to have breakfast in the hotel restaurant. They had a buffet spread; everything from omelets to waffles and pancakes. Jada and I had the waffles. Malcolm had eggs and toast. He was all smiles as he reminisced about how great it was to finally get to eat some good food. I was so glad my husband could smile after all he had been through. Hallelujah, thank you Jesus!

I didn't know if he was smiling so hard because of the food or because he got to spend the whole day with me yesterday.

We hurried back to the room to get dressed for church.

"I hope you're not too tired after morning service. I want to attend Pastor Nehemiah Washington's church in High Point this afternoon. They are having evening service and I want to surprise him," he said.

"Sure honey, that will be great. I'm sure he will be so surprised to see you. Trust me, I don't care where we go as long as I'm with you," I happily replied.

I had to admit, it still felt like a dream. And if that weren't enough, Grace texted me.

**DID YOU REMEMBER UR NOT ON
ANY BIRTH CONTROL?**

Why this was the first thing this chick was thinking about this morning, I didn't know but I responded back.

**I DIDN'T KNOW I WAS GOING TO NEED ANY
BIRTH CONTROL! I DIDN'T KNOW I WAS
COMING TO SEE MY HUSBAND WHO JUST
GOT OUT OF PRISON.**

Leave it to Grace! She responded back with:

**WELL IT'S NOT LIKE HE'S NOT YOUR HUS-
BAND BUT HOW COOL WOULD THAT BE IF
YOU WERE PREGGO!**

I responded:

**BUT NOW THAT WE'RE TALKING ABOUT IT,
IF IT HAPPENS THEN SO BE IT!**

She fired back with:

OK MAMA BEAR

I didn't have time to think about what would happen if I were pregnant. I knew I'd be happy though because it would be mine and Malcolm's and we would love and provide a life for it that we didn't have; a life with two stable parents. I hadn't realized it but everything stopped when Malcolm got locked up. I stopped hoping, dreaming, and thinking about what our lives would be like because our lives were incomplete without him. We were all just existing from one day to the next until he could be with us again.

We finished dressing and met Jada in the parking lot. We arrived in the church parking lot at 11:20 a.m. on the dot. I didn't realize it until I saw the building but I really missed coming here with Malcolm. The parking lot was filled on both sides of the church as usual. Both the Pastor and First Lady's car's were in their respective spaces. I could tell that Jada was excited to be at her home church again too.

As we entered the vestibule, the greeters recognized us, hugged us and greeted us with joy! One of the male greeters gave Malcom a great embrace and started praising the Lord right there for Malcolm's presence in the building. I guess it carried over because as we entered the packed sanctuary before we could even get seated, Malcolm left jada and me and just took off running. Then Jada started dancing in the Holy Spirit. The Pastor got up out of his seat and said, *"I know that isn't Brother Malcolm running?"*

He kept watching as Malcolm rounded the corner near the front of the church and he got a better glimpse. Then he said, *"Lord, it is Brother Malcolm who was wrongfully incarcerated!"* Pastor Murphy made his way down to the floor from the pulpit and when Malcolm rounded that front corner the third time, he grabbed Malcolm and the two of them started dancing in the Spirit! And this was how the service started. The musicians got on their instruments and the praise party continued. People started running and dancing all over the building. The musicians were jamming! It was a Holy Spirit frenzy. People were praising and thanking the Lord.

I was so overwhelmed I didn't know what to do. Tears of joy streamed down my face. I don't know what got into me but before I knew it, I too was dancing in the Holy Spirit. Malcolm came and grabbed my hand, and we danced and praised God together! I had never experienced anything like that before.

The service carried on from the praise break with praise and worship and the choir singing a song that was fire. Pastor Murphy preached an awesome word. I liked the church in Massachusetts and even though it had been three years since we'd been here, the New Cathedral of Jerusalem really felt like home. I was really starting to realize how great this God of ours was! I was beginning to understand what it felt like to know can't nobody do me like Jesus! This weekend couldn't have happened without the Lord.

We were at church for a while after it was over. Everyone wanted to hug Malcolm or shake his hand. Some of their family members had been locked up with him and he'd been an encouragement for them in the prison ministry. It was like he was a celebrity. When we finally left church we were all famished. After all that praising, we had worked up an appetite. So we decided to go to the Golden Corral Buffet.

I knew Malcolm said we'd be meeting Mrs. Yancey at the bank in the morning but I wanted to spend more time with her so I asked if we could stop by and visit her on our way to Pastor Nehemiah's church. I couldn't imagine how she was doing knowing her husband of forty years would never be coming home again. Malcolm thought that was a great idea so I stepped out to call her and make sure she would be home.

"Hello darling," Mrs. Yancey answered.

I had to laugh because she always answered her phone on the first ring.

"Hello Mrs. Yancey," I replied.

Mrs. Yancey said, *"I was hoping you would call me. Isn't it a blessing to be with your husband?"*

"Yes ma'am, it sure is," I replied.

I wished Mrs. Yancey could see the big smile on my face through the phone.

"I'm so happy for you baby," she said.

"Mrs. Yancey, do you need anything," I asked.

"Thank you for asking, baby but I'm fine. I'm packing up the house as best I can. The movers are coming this afternoon to box up all my china and everything else that I'm taking with me to Florida. I plan to be moved all out within the next two weeks," she said.

"I know we're going to see you in the morning but I was hoping we could come visit you today," I asked.

"Irene, that would be lovely. I would like that very much," she replied.

"Ok great. We're eating now so we'll come over after when we're finished," I told her.

"I look forward to it. Bye now," she said.

"See you soon Mrs. Yancey," I replied.

When I got back to the table, Malcolm and Jada had their faces in their plates. Malcolm was throwing down. He was eating way too fast though. Then I remembered that they were rushed to eat in prison. I didn't let it bother me too much. I was sure Malcolm would re-adjust to being a civilian again.

"Is she home," Malcolm asked?

161

"Yes she is and she would be delighted if we would come by and see her. I told her we'd probably come after we ate if that's ok," I answered.

"Cool," he said as he stuffed another piece of cornbread in his mouth.

I was glad we were already eating in case Mrs. Yancey asked. I remembered all too well that she was not a very good cook. Were it not for my Mother teaching me, we would have surely bankrupted them eating takeout.

We finished our meal and headed out. We were all full enough to pop.

Jada said, "I'm glad we're going to visit Mrs. Yancey because if I went back to the room, I would surely be going straight to sleep!"

"I would like to sis," I chimed in.

"Well I am much too excited to be tired just yet. I'm sure I'll feel it later though," Malcolm said.

I texted Mrs. Yancey and let her know we were on our way. When we arrived at Mrs. Yancey's home, the Mercedes truck and the Lexus that Mr. Yancey left Malcolm were parked in the driveway. It had been three years but I remembered everything about the big five bedroom house with its huge kitchen, big backyard, and the 8 ft in ground pool. And it was all left to us. I still couldn't believe it. Jada had never seen the house before. She was blown away.

Mrs. Yancey answered the door as she always did; with a big smile on her face. She hugged each of us as we walked through the huge double doors into the foyer; the same foyer we stood in that fateful night before Malcolm had to turn himself in. It all came flooding back.

"Come in and have a seat please. Make yourselves at home," she said and winked at us as she excused herself for a moment. She led us into the living room to sit down.

Malcolm whispered, *"Well officially tomorrow this will be our home."*

I could faintly hear Mrs. Yancey in the laundry room. It sounded like she was putting clothes from the washer to the dryer.

Jada whispered, *"The furniture in here looks quite dated for a home as beautiful as this."*

"Don't be fooled. All of this furniture cost a lot of money. Decorating this house was Mrs. Yancey's pride and joy," I remarked.

Shortly Mrs. Yancey joined us in the living room.

"Can I offer you something to drink," she asked.

"No ma'am," we all responded together like the Hallelujah Chorus.

"I'm so glad you all came to visit me today," she said, still smiling.

We introduced her officially to Jada. She'd spoken to her several times on the phone but this was their first time getting to see each other in person. Mrs. Yancey glided seamlessly from one conversation to another. There were no silent moments. She even cracked a few jokes and had us bursting at the seams in laughter. I was so happily surprised at how she seemed to be getting along after Mr. Yancey's passing just last week. Mrs. Yancey kept saying, *"Mr. Yancey had his faults, but he always treated me with respect."*

I felt sorry for her. I thought to myself, *"That Mr. Yancey was Dr. Jekyll and Mr. Hyde."* Mr. Yancey didn't respect her at all. He always gave her what she wanted because it was his penance for her putting up with him knowing he was a pedophile and a sexual predator who got away with too much.

Mrs. Yancey offered to show Malcolm all of the house that he had inherited. He was so gracious. He told her that there would be plenty of time for that and that he knew she was packing up so he didn't want to disrupt anything. That was my Malcolm; always thoughtful and considerate.

Then she said, *"Mr. Yancey and I discussed and decided that you should receive the house and all the furniture. It's a large house to have to fill all at one time so we felt if we left you mostly everything then you all could keep what you wanted and replace what you didn't a little at a time. We purchased a new mattress for you for the master bedroom and all the bedding, linens, and towels have been laundered for you with a couple of new pieces thrown in."*

"Thank you Mrs. Yancey. I have to say we certainly didn't expect any of this and we really haven't even had a chance to process it," Malcolm replied.

"Well officially after tomorrow everything will be yours to do with as you please. I wasn't sure if you were going to keep the house or sell it but you'll meet Mr. Flounders who has handled our finances for years. We wanted him to set you up so that you will have your wealth for a long time. And his sons and daughters are in business with him in case you prefer someone closer to your age. They'll be transferring all of the money to the accounts of your choosing and signing over the deeds to both houses and the titles to the cars."

"Wow, Mrs. Yancey. I don't know what to say," Malcolm said, sliding to the edge of his chair.

"Malcolm," she continued. *"I can't express to you the impact your letters had on Mr. Yancey. After a few of them he started doing some extensive research on you. He found out from some professor friends of his at North Carolina A&T that you were so talented you were slated to go high in the NFL draft three years ago and you would have made millions. He also spoke with some local news sport reporters here in Greensboro that followed your career. They told him that you were a very special player with a lot of promise. He felt terrible that he'd let his ego get in the way of ruining your life and he wanted to do his best to make amends. That's why this all is yours* along with the house in Myrtle Beach, the cars and the money. I just need about two weeks to get through the holidays and I'll be all packed up and moved out."

Malcolm got up and went and put his arms around Mrs. Yancey. Jada and I were already a mess of tears.

He told her, *"Take all the time you need. There is no rush. We're going to head back to Massachusetts probably until June when the school year is over for John and Abby. And that gives us time as well to decide how we're going to transition back to Greensboro."*

"You are too kind. I see why my Irene loves you so much," she replied.

I got up and went over to hug her as well.

"I love you Mrs. Yancey," I managed to muster out through my tears.

"I love you too Irene. I always have and I always will," she replied.

We all collected ourselves and Malcolm said, *"We don't want to take up the rest of your afternoon. We just wanted to come by and see you today. We didn't know how much time we'd get to spend with you tomorrow."*

"I'm so glad you did. I can give you the keys to the summer home in Myrtle Beach. I never liked the beach and all that sand. Don't get me wrong, the home is beautiful but not too much my style. I never made too big a fuss about it because we only went for a couple of weeks every year. I preferred to spend the rest of our vacation visiting my sisters. On the advice of Mr. Flounders, we started renting it out because it stayed empty most of the year and it generates quite a bit of income that will now also be all yours," she said as she got up and walked towards the huge fireplace. She had a beautiful vase that adorned it.

Then she asked, *"Have you ever been on a yacht?"*

"No ma'am," we all chimed in again and burst into another fit of laughter.

She lifted up the bottom of the vase to reveal what looked like lots of keys inside. She grabbed them and walked back over to us.

"I got on one one time and it scared me almost to death. It was too much water but you guys should go on one at least once when you're there. You're young. You might actually enjoy it," she said and handed the keys to Malcolm.

She continued, *"These are the keys to this house, the summer home, and the cars. The summer home also has a code but all of that is written down with the paperwork you'll receive in the morning. So, I will see you at 9 a.m. downtown at the BB&T on Green Street,"* she asked.

"We will see you then," Malcolm responded as we all stood up and headed toward the front door. We hugged Mrs. Yancey again and headed to the car.

Jada said, *"Guys, I'm going to sit the next service out. I'm pooped. You can drop me off back at the hotel."*

It was a little after 5 p.m.

Mrs. Yancey heard Jada and said, *"Lord you young uns can stay in church all day. Are you going back to your church's evening service,"* she asked.

Malcolm didn't quite remember the name of the church, but he knew it was in High Point.

Mrs. Yancy asked, *"Who is the Pastor?"*

We forgot how connected they were and that they knew a lot of people.

Malcolm said, *"Bishop Nehemiah Washington, Sr."*

"Oh, that's Pastor Washington Jr's father. I know them well. That Bishop Washington is a nice man and a preaching man of God. I heard he'd retired and gave the church over to his eldest son. Well you guys have a good time now, she said."

"Thank you Mrs. Yancey," we all chimed in again and waved to her goodbye.

I didn't realize how much I missed Mrs. Yancey until I saw her. I was so grateful for the time I got to spend with her and even more grateful that she was a part of our lives.

We stopped by the hotel to drop Jada off. We went in to use the bathroom and freshen up too. Jada said she was going to take a nap and she'd see us when we got back. We jumped back in the car and headed to church.

Chapter Sixteen

Malcolm managed to find the name of the church before we left the hotel so that we could put the directions into the GPS. Their service started at 6 p.m. and we were about fifteen minutes late. Praise & worship had already begun by the time we arrived and walked in. The usher greeted us and escorted us to our seats. She walked us up only a few rows from the front of the church. As we walked to our seats, I noticed the women eyeing Malcolm down like he was new meat at a meat market. I knew we were in church but those strumpets better go somewhere!

Right before praise & worship ended the Bishop, Pastor Nehemiah's Father, came out first and sat in the pulpit. Then another man in a robe came out and everyone stood up. Once he sat down in the pulpit, everyone sat back down.

Malcolm leaned over to me and whispered in my ear, *"That is Pastor Nehemiah."*

I looked up at that man, down at the floor, and then I looked up again. I started shaking. I was in complete shock.

I pinched Malcolm and said, *"I want to leave now."*

Malcom asked, *"What's wrong?"*

Still shaking, I replied, *"Malcolm, that Pastor Nehemiah Washington is Mr. Nathan, my Father!"*

I couldn't believe my eyes.

Malcolm whispered back, *"Are you serious?"*

I would know that tall, handsome, dark skinned man anywhere. He had put on some gray but there he was, my father, Mr. Nathan live and in living color.

"Malcolm, this man is my Father," I replied.

Malcolm whispered again, *"Not that I don't believe you baby but are you sure? This man is married with two children. He never mentioned anything to me about a previous family."*

I snapped back, *"Oh well, his kids are my siblings. Look at him, you never thought that he looked like John? They are the spitting image of each other. I can't stay here. I need to go."*

I couldn't believe this man had abandoned my Mother, John, Abby, and I, and now he was a Pastor.

I was ready to leave but Malcolm said, *"We can't leave now baby. There is too much that needs to be resolved. I am your husband. Do you trust me?"*

I nodded, *"Yes,"* but the tears had already begun to flow down my face.

"I'm going to handle this," he promised.

We stayed until the service was just about over. The hardest thing I ever had to do in my life was to sit and listen to that no good, lying, son-of-a-bitch preach. I looked down at the floor or my hands through the entire service when Malcolm wasn't holding my hand. Towards the end of the service, the Deacons came up to take up the offering. Everyone was asked to walk up to the offering basket and deposit their offering in the basket. I told Malcolm I wasn't walking up there so he left me sitting, walked up to the basket, and gave his offering. That was when Pastor Nehemiah, my father, noticed him. He stood up and waved to

Malcolm. Malcolm nodded and waved back.

After the offering, Mr. Nathan stood up and asked that all the visitors please stand up and introduce themselves. Malcolm stood up and my father walked over to him and asked everyone to give Malcolm an applause because he was an ideal inmate at the Caledonia Prison who was just released. Still not recognizing who I was sitting next to Malcolm, my father asked Malcolm to say a few words. He walked toward Malcolm and handed him the microphone. Malcolm began his dissertation.

"I give God the honor and praise for getting me released from prison for something that I should never have received such a harsh penalty for as a first time offender. I give honor to Bishop Nehemiah Sr. and Pastor Nehemiah Jr. who prayed for me through my three years in prison. I give honor to my wife, Mrs. Irene Hampton Austin whom I've loved practically all my life and who has been my rock during the most challenging time of both our lives. And my wife..."

He looks at me and says, *"Stand up baby."* I could have kicked Malcolm in his leg! I didn't want to stand but I did. I didn't look up though. My eyes were plastered to the floor.

Malcolm continued, *"...my wife who has just made me aware Pastor Nehemiah, that you are her father."*

There was a gasp and then a silence from the entire congregation.

Malcolm looked at Pastor Nehemiah and asked, *"Do you remember your daughter Irene?"*

Mr. Nathan didn't respond. I had finally looked up to look him in his face. He looked like he'd seen a ghost.

Malcolm continued, *"Pastor Washington actually has three children. Irene has a younger brother and sister as well whom he abandoned many years ago."*

At that point The Bishop stood up and asked Malcolm, *"Son, what are you talking about?"*

Malcolm responded, *"God bless you Bishop. My apologies but I couldn't leave without rectifying this situation for my wife. I have interacted with your son for three years now in the prison ministry and never knew until today that the man I held in such high regard and spoke to my wife about weekly was actually her estranged father. Bishop, this is your granddaughter."*

Malcolm was pointing at me! I could have kicked him again.

The Bishop looked at me and said, *"Young lady, will you come here to me?"*

Malcolm grabbed my hand and we walked up front. My heart was pounding so hard I thought that everyone around me could hear it. The congregation was staring hard at us but no one said a word.

Once I reached the pulpit the Bishop came down from the podium. He walked towards me, put his hands on my shoulders, and looked me square in the face. I'm guessing he was looking to see if there was any resemblance but my Mother always told me that I looked just like my father.

He turned me around, pointed to Mr. Nathan, and said, *"You're saying this man is your father?"*

I replied, *"Yes sir he is."*

An older lady with a big hat sitting on the other side of the church stands up and says *"Bishop, let's be for real. That is not our son's daughter!"*

The Bishop says to her, *"Please have a seat. I am taking care of this. We need to get to the bottom of this accusation. If our son indeed has other children, this affects us all."*

She didn't like it. Her face was filled with anger and then embarrassment but she sat down immediately.

Mr. Nathan would not look at me at all. The Bishop asked him, *"My son, how do you respond to this accusation? Is this your daughter? I'm looking at her and she looks just like you!"*

Then Mr. Nathan finally looks up at me, then he looks at his father and says, *"Yes Bishop."*

The lady with the big hat yelled, *"Nehemiah!"*

The congregation gasped again. The Bishop then says to the congregation, *"Everyone standing. We are dismissing you all from the service so that we can continue this matter privately. May God bless you and we will see you this week for our regularly scheduled services. Pastor Nehemiah, please come join us up front."*

There was another lady with a little boy looking at me like she was crazy along with whom I assumed was grandmother but I didn't care. My father was perpetrating a lie all these years because he is married. He left my Mother with Abby, John and me!

The Bishop continued, *"Your husband said there are more of you?"*

"Yes...," I replied. *"...a sister named Abby and a brother named John. Our Mother is deceased due to pneumonia and complications from H.I.V. which she got from her addiction to crack and heroin thanks to this man who left her strung out and then disappeared. All this time we were told to call him Mr. Nathan by our Mother. I never knew that the man my husband spoke to me so highly about every week was this man until I walked in and saw him today."*

I told them the whole story.

The Bishop looked at Mr. Nathan and said, *"Son if this is true, you will have to step down as the Pastor of this church leaving me to have to resume as acting interim Pastor until such time as I can find a suitable replacement."*

There was no response from Mr. Nathan.

The Bishop continued, *"Son you have brought scandal to the house of the Lord. Do you have nothing to say?"*

Mr. Nathan finally mustered a weak, *"I'm so sorry."*

The Bishop replied, *"Don't apologize to me. You need to apologize to your children whom you abandoned. Then you need to* apologize to your wife whom I'm sure had no idea of the goings on of your sordid past and is sitting over there hurt."

Then the Bishop asked my Father, *"Are there any more children you have out there in the world that you've abandoned and not told us about?"*

My grandfather was giving Mr. Nathan the business. I loved him already.

"No sir," he responded.

At that point, Mr. Nathan's wife stood up, grabbed the boy sitting next to her and walked out of the church crying.

The Bishop motions to my grandmother to go after her.

The Bishop continued, *"Young lady I cannot begin to apologize to you for the injustices done to you and your family by my son. But we believe in reconciliation and restoration. This was all a big shock to our family and we all need time to bring more clarity to this situation. Are you willing to allow us the opportunity to make as much of this right as we can?"*

"Yes sir," I responded.

We exchanged numbers and he asked if I could bring Abby and John to meet them as well. He said he wanted to have an official event to welcome us to the Washington family. Although by the looks of my grandmother, I was sure we'd all have to pass a DNA test for her.

He looked at Mr. Nathan again and said, *"You need to fix this."* Then he reached out his arms. I felt safe enough to allow the embrace which was very short.

"Alright then," he turned and walked behind the pulpit and exited out that door.

Only Malcolm, Mr. Nathan, and I were left standing in the sanctuary. Mr. Nathan leaned forward and tried to give me a hug.

"No," I yelled, pulling away. *"What makes you think I want to hug you? I needed your hugs all of my life. You are a fraud and a*

fake and have been nothing more than an absentee father for all these years. You left my Mother strung out and you just abandoned us. My Mother died from A.I.D.S. because of you. You meant everything to her. She asked you for help and you bounced!"

Tears of hurt and disgust ran down my face. I looked up at Malcolm, *"I'm ready to go. I can't stand to look at this man any longer."*

Malcolm grabbed my hand and escorted me out of the building. Once he got me in the car, I cried the entire drive back to the hotel.

"It's going to be alright baby, I promise. All we have to do is keep trusting God. He hasn't brought us this far to leave us," he said.

His words were comforting. When we finally arrived back at the hotel, I was exhausted. I took off my clothes and laid across the bed.

Malcolm rubbed my back. I could tell he felt so bad about how the afternoon turned out. He was so excited to introduce me to the man who had been so instrumental in helping him get through the last three years of his life. Neither of us could have ever imagined the afternoon would turn out this way.

"I can't believe that this Friday is Christmas," he said.

"I know," I said, trying to sound happy.

"Well from this day forth, you and I will never be separated again," he said.

Before I knew it, I was smiling that huge smile that Malcolm always managed to get out of me.

"There's that million dollar smile I've missed," he said.

Only he could make me smile and forget all of my troubles. My thoughts were all over the place. I kept seeing Mr. Nathan's face, my grandfather's face, and my grandmother's face.

"I'm sorry Malcolm," I said.

"Irene, you have nothing to be sorry about," he replied.

"But I do. I took your Pastor Washington away from you," I responded, sadly.

"You nor I had any idea that this man was your father. It doesn't take away what he did for me there but this is now. I couldn't ignore your pain. We are together now and we will face all of our problems head on together," he said.

I knew that was his stand on it but somehow needing to hear it made all the difference.

"Baby, what would you say about us asking Mrs. Yancey to come with us to Massachusetts for Christmas," he asked.

I sat up and gave him a huge hug.

He continued, "She said she needed two weeks to be out but the thought of her spending Christmas alone just doesn't sit right with me."

"Oh Malcolm! I certainly don't have a problem with that. Nothing would make me happier," I replied.

He was so wise.

"It's settled then. We will ask her tomorrow," he said with a huge grin on his face.

That was just like Malcolm. He seemed just as happy as me about the idea.

"What about Jada," I asked. "I want her there too?"

"Leave that to me. You know she'll do anything for her little brother," he said and commenced grabbing my cell phone and calling her.

I could tell she asked him how church was because he told her about what happened. It sounded like she asked if I needed her to come over but he told her that we were beat and that we were going to turn in for the night. He told her we'd be ready at 8:30 a.m. to leave for the bank and then told her good nite.

So much happened this weekend that I was sure we'd remember it for the rest of our lives!

Monday morning came quickly. We were up and headed to meet Mrs. Yancey at the bank at 9 a.m. The process didn't take long at all for the transfers of the deed to the house and the cars to Malcolm. The money was transferred into Malcolm's account to which he added my name jointly. He transferred the million he'd promised Jada into her account. I think she was the happiest of us all. Malcolm and I were still in shock.

Malcolm snapped out of it long enough to ask Mrs. Yancey if she would accompany us to Massachusetts for Christmas. She was only too thrilled to say yes. We told her we'd come by and discuss the details with her later. We had to activate Malcolm's cell phone and then to drop Jada off at the airport. She planned to drive down on Thursday. She was so overwhelmed she cried and praised God all the way to the airport. She cried until she had me crying. Finally, we were crying tears of joy. No, the money didn't erase the pain we'd all been through but it gave us hope for a future that would make us forget the pain.

We returned the rental car and took the Uber to Mrs. Yancey's. We would be driving one of our newly owned cars back to Massachusetts. I called my job and requested the week off for a family emergency. I chose to wait until I could sit face to face with John and Abby to tell them about Mr. Nathan. I wondered how they would feel about it. I wasn't even sure they remembered him. I just wanted to enjoy Malcolm being home and Mrs. Yancey being back in our lives before I introduced the Washington's into our lives.

I was getting ready to make reservations at the hotel in town for Mrs. Yancey. All of us would not sleep comfortably in our three bed-room home. Mrs. Yancey wouldn't hear of it. She wanted to stay with us. So we decided that Malcolm and I would sleep on the pull out couch in the living room and give Mrs. Yancey mine and Abby's bed. We'd buy a blow up bed for Abby and John to sleep in Grace's room and we would give Jada John's room.

All I knew was that Christmas was going to be joyous and fun this year. A lot of those past holidays when my Mother was alive were not festive at all. Abby, John and I had learned to take the bitter with the sweet. This year would be sweet for sure. We would finally all be under one roof - Malcolm, Jada, Grace, Mrs Yancey, Abby, John and I. I hoped Grace would be just as excited as I was because I was going to ask her to prepare our Christmas day dinner. I was so glad that Malcolm thought of inviting Mrs. Yancey. She had always been family to me but now that Mr. Yancey was gone she seemed like family even more now for real. It was her that we connected with. It was her that we loved the most. I had come to admire Mrs. Yancey. She was a strong Black woman.

Chapter Seventeen

On Christmas Eve our house was full. We had a Christmas tree up and decorated with candlelights all around the house. Abby and I did the decorations. Dale and Rodney, two of Malcolm's longtime friends, drove up to Massachusetts to be with us as well. Mrs. Yancey made some Christmas cookies. We all knew Mrs. Yancey could cook but John found his way right back beside her in the kitchen just like old times. We had a huge Uno game going on at the kitchen table. The house was really loud with joy and laughter and I, for one, was happy to hear it.

The kitchen was filled with the aroma of a whole turkey, a glazed ham, lasagna, string beans, rice and gravy, and stuffing. Grace really outdid herself. I could wait because come noon tomorrow, we would be throwing down and I couldn't wait. I already had to threaten John because he had been trying to get into the food early.

It had been a whirlwind of a week. We drove back to Massachusetts because we brought Mrs. Yancey with us instead of putting her on a train even though she said she didn't mind the scenery. Malcolm just wouldn't hear of it. Grace, Abby, and

John were all too thrilled to be getting Malcolm and Mrs. Yancey home for Christmas. I was surprised but thankful how Malcolm and Grace have been getting along. We had lots of talks about Grace and her sexual preferences while Malcolm was locked up. His instructions were always for me to keep an eye on her but she'd proven to be loyal to us as a family and another sister to me especially while he was away. This softened him up a little because he was not feeling Grace for some time. Malcolm appreciated her loyalty and he told me how the Lord had somewhat changed his heart and given him more compassion concerning gays and lesbians. He and Grace seemed really cool now.

Malcolm shared with me the story of this eighteen year old young black guy who was sent to prison for gunning down his cousin in a blackout. The young man was gay and fragile and a lot of inmates picked on him constantly. The kid never had any peace. Malcolm said that he was not feeling the young man until Pastor Nehemiah stood up for the kid. He said that Mr. Nehemiah preached a word saying that God had saved all of us from something and he told the inmates to leave the kid alone. Malcolm became convicted, then he repented and befriended the young man. He said the young man shared with him that he was beaten and raped from the age of 6 years old until fourteen by his mother's boyfriend. He ran away at fourteen and out in the streets he became an alcoholic. During that time he said he lived in different people's homes and many nights at the homeless shelter. Malcolm felt sorry for him and he tried to introduce Jesus to him. He said the young man did not think that Jesus cared about a person like him. Malcolm was able to witness to him and the young man gave his life to Christ.

I was so glad to see Abby, Grace, and John when I got back home. I hadn't been away from them since we moved to

Massachusetts. Malcolm and I sat down with them and told them about everything that transpired while we were in North Carolina. Of course, I also had to tell John and Abby about our Father. They didn't seem fazed at all which I guess was a good thing given the fact that they didn't even remember him. I asked them how they felt about allowing him access to our lives now. Abby thought it would be extremely awkward. John just wanted to know if it meant he'd be getting more gifts and presents for birthdays and Christmas. I should have expected as much. I couldn't blame them. I was still processing how I felt about it all. I mean I've practiced forgiving him every day since we saw him but I guess it's going to take some time for us all.

Jada was the only one missing from our Christmas Eve get-together. She had gone out to dinner with some friends she'd not seen since she left Amherst. Malcolm rented a bunch of rooms at the hotel downtown Amherst. He thought Mrs. Yancey and Jada would stay there but they wouldn't hear of it. So he just got rooms for Dale and Rodney because everyone wanted to be all together at the house. So we bought a pull-out bed for the living room. Grace gave Mrs. Yancey her room. Jada slept in John's room. Grace and Abby took the pull-out which left John on the couch. I'm sure, were it not for the fact that Malcolm and Mrs. Yancey were there, that he would not have been happy away from his precious PS5 but he graciously gave up his room. I told him there was still hope for him yet! Abby even allowed Josh to come over.

Jada walked through the door three minutes before midnight. Our house was finally filled with everyone we called our family and we loved. I didn't remember Christmas ever being this festive for our family. There was so much love and laughter that I could tell everyone was having a great time.

At the stroke of midnight, everyone yelled Merry Christmas! Then started the hugs and kisses. Malcolm asked everyone to gather in the living room so we could have a prayer of thanks. We all migrated one by one into a circle in the living room and grabbed each other's hands.

"Lord, I thank you for your grace and mercy. I thank you that we are all alive and able to witness another Christmas season together. I thank you for Lord for being released from prison after almost three years. I'm thankful especially for my wife Irene and for my brother and sisters Abby, John, and Jada. I thank you Lord for Grace and Mrs. Yancey being with us and for my friends Dale and Rodney for coming to be with us as well. I thank you Lord for Abby's boyfriend Josh."

At this point in his prayer Malcolm started crying. His crying started to make me cry. I was holding his hand so I couldn't wipe my face so I tried to wipe my cheek on my clothes and as I looked over, I saw Jada and Mrs. Yancey crying. Abby and Josh were crying as well. Josh surprised me but we were all so grateful that we couldn't help but cry tears of joy.

Malcolm continued, *"Lord I thank you for keeping us together from this time forward and that nothing ever again causes us to be a part. Our father which art in heaven, hallowed be thy name. Thy kingdom come. Thy will be done in earth as it is in heaven. Give us this day our daily bread. And forgive us our trespasses as we forgive those who trespass against us. And lead us not into temptation, but deliver us from evil: For thine is the kingdom, and the power, and the glory for ever. Amen."*

The prayer ended and Dale and Rodney lightened the mood by teasing Malcolm about his long prayers. They said that Malcolm used to pray long prayers before their games at A&T. He would have all the players choked up before the game but they played their hearts out afterwards.

Then Malcolm's phone rang. We all wondered who in the world could be calling at this late hour. It was Mr. Nathan. He wanted to call and wish us a Merry Christmas and catch up with all of us. It was too soon for me still. I couldn't bring myself to speak to him. Heck, I was still wrapping my head around the fact that his name was Nehemiah and not Nathan. I had forgiven him because I understood that I had to do that for me and so that I would be right in the sight of God but I had to ask everyday because every time I thought about it I was mad all over again.

Malcolm said, *"Give your Father a chance."*

"Time," is all I could reply. *"Just give me some time."*

***

On May 1, 2021, five years and three days after our Mother's death, we gathered at the cemetery to put a headstone on my Mother's grave. The day she died was the hardest day of my life but at this moment I felt as though she was smiling down on us. It had been my desire since we buried her to a headstone over her grave. With our new found fortune, we were finally able to fulfill my desire. My Mother deserved at least that and with everything we'd been through, I finally felt at peace.

We stayed in Massachusetts to allow John and Abby to finish out their school year. Malcolm and I had been back and forth to Greensboro looking for a place to live. We planned to move back as soon as the school year was over. After what Abby had been through in the Yancey's house, that was the last place we were going to bring her to live. Even though the house had been signed over to us, we still told Mrs. Yancey that we were going to sell it. She understood. We let the personal finance people Mrs. Yancey gave us handle the sale of the house. We were even able to get Grace to sell her house because she wasn't going to live in it either. She said she would wait to see where we were moving and then she would find someplace nearby. I made her promise that because I was five months pregnant and I would need all the support I could get.

Malcolm had been awesome since he'd been home from prison. He was busy every day making plans for our future. He was so excited about the baby. We didn't know what we were having yet but Malcolm was intent on finding us a place before our September due date. He made sure we scheduled monthly calls with my father, Mr. Nehemiah, who had actually been pretty consistent since I accidentally found him. He filled in some of the missing pieces of what happened between him and my Mother.

Malcolm suggested we make a small ceremony out of the headstone placing. He brought a dozen roses to lay over the headstone just like he did when we first laid my Mother to rest. He also got a soloist from our church to sing my favorite song, my soul has been anchored, for us. I took pictures on my cell phone of the new headstone. Malcolm prayed before we left. The celebration was so beautiful.

We walked back to the limo Malcolm rented while the soloist was still singing. A black Lexus SUV with tinted windows pulled up behind the Limo as we were getting in. It was our Father, Pastor Nehemiah Washington. He came to the limo and hugged John and Abby. He shook Malcolm's hand and hugged him. I didn't know he knew we were out there. Malcolm probably told him. I hadn't expected him.

He came to me last and said, *"Hello Beautiful. Your Mother used to call you that."*

Then he walked over to my Mother's grave and kneeled down. We could see him weeping. He seemed really sincere and I was moved with compassion. I didn't know if it was my hormones because of the baby or if the Holy Spirit was moving in me.

I told Malcolm, *"I'll be right back."*

I got out of the limo, went back to the grave, and put my arms around my Father as he wept. At that moment I decided that I would allow him that privilege; to be my father. I knew my Mother would want that too.

The soloist continued to sing, *"my soul is anchored in the Lord."* Mine was too.

Made in United States
Orlando, FL
02 May 2023

32710009R00112